365 DAYS

CATHY CARR

365
DAYS TO
ALASKA

TO ALASKA

AMULET BOOKS
NEW YORK

For my father,
my first and best teacher

Cataloging-in-Publication Data has been applied for and may be obtained from the Library of Congress.

ISBN 978-1-4197-4380-1

Text copyright © 2021 Cathy Carr
Illustrations copyright © 2021 Maeve Norton
Book design by Marcie Lawrence

Printed and bound in U.S.A.
10 9 8 7 6 5 4 3 2

Amulet Books are available at special discounts when purchased in quantity for premiums and promotions as well as fundraising or educational use. Special editions can also be created to specification. For details, contact specialsales@abramsbooks.com or the address below.

Amulet Books® is a registered trademark of Harry N. Abrams, Inc.

ABRAMS The Art of Books
195 Broadway, New York, NY 10007
abramsbooks.com

Chapter 1

Rigel put the tip of the hunting knife into the hare's belly and made a careful slit.

Once there was a hole in the fur, she could work her fingers in and pull the pelt right off, like turning a glove inside out. Then it was time to lay the pelt over a nearby branch and finish field-dressing the hare.

A raven landed in a nearby spruce tree with a heavy flap. It studied Rigel, its head to one side, then hopped to a lower branch for a better look. It was probably waiting for her to finish gutting the hare and throw its goodies into the scrub. Rigel would bet it had seen hunters do that before. It might have seen her doing it before. Ravens remembered things.

"Hello," Rigel said to it.

The raven riffled its feathers. It offered her a croak—not a long, loud *cr-r-ruck*; a shorter, softer *ah-ah*.

Rigel always spoke to ravens. It would have seemed rude not to, they were so smart.

The cleaned hare and its rolled-up skin went into Rigel's pack. She tossed the innards, head, and feet under the spruce where the raven sat. She squatted by the stream to clean the buck knife, then put it back into its sheath. She rinsed her hands quickly in the icy water, wiped them on her hoodie, and went back for the pack and gun. Then Rigel checked the safety on the .22 and put it over her arm in a cradle carry, the way her dad, Bear, had taught her.

"Enjoy," she said to the raven before turning away. She'd noticed waitresses in restaurants said that when they put your food down. Not that Rigel ate in restaurants very often, but she was no hick. She'd been to Fairbanks.

She headed home along the stream.

Rigel was bringing home two hares, not bad for her first time out. Two was enough for a meal for the five of them. She hoped her mother would make a casserole. Lila's rabbit casserole was the best. Bear always said that, even nowadays, when he had almost nothing else nice to say about Lila.

And Rigel had proven Bear was right when he argued last week that she was old enough to hunt on her own, that she had a good head on her shoulders. "She's eleven years old," he'd said, and Lila had answered, "You know, some people would say she's *only* eleven." For a moment there, Rigel had been afraid they were going to start fighting, on her birthday. But she shoved that memory away. The point was, she had gone out and taken her time and done everything exactly right, and now she was bringing home meat.

If it had been winter, Rigel would have walked back to the cabin on the frozen stream, which was quicker. But breakup had come early this year, and now in mid-May, the ice was already gone. She walked along the trail at the top of the sandy bank instead. She got glimpses of their cabin through the trees and brush as she went along, and started catching snatches of voices. Her sisters were outside.

Izzy's voice came first. Izzy was only five and her high, bright voice carried easily. Willow's voice came later, because it was soft and low. Rigel hoped her voice would sound that nice when she was fourteen.

"Rye Bear!" Izzy threw down her jump rope and ran to her. "Did you get anything?"

Rigel twitched her nose and munched with her mouth, the way a hare would.

"Rabbits!" Izzy shouted. "Rabbit rabbit rabbit rabbit rabbit!"

She bunny-hopped beside Rigel all the way back to the cabin.

Hare, not rabbit, Lila would have said. She had a degree in biology and could be picky about that stuff. *Hare, rabbit, it's the same thing,* that's what Bear would have said. Rigel didn't correct Izzy. She swatted one of Izzy's sunshine-yellow braids instead and Izzy laughed and whirled away. Her real name was Iris, but that name only got used when she was in trouble.

They had a good-sized cabin, ten logs high, with two rooms. There was one window on each side of the front door, and the door and window trim were painted red. The red was pretty against the weathered brown logs, and there was a bench under each window, where you could sit on nice days. The dried head of a northern pike was nailed to the cabin door, jaws spread open to show all of its long, sharp teeth. Wilfred Thompson, one of Bear's old hunting buddies from Fort McPhee, had put that up when the Harman family moved out here. He told them to not take it down, and they never touched it.

Willow was sitting on a bench with a stack of her magazines. She'd already read them all and torn out pictures for the collages she liked to make, but it seemed like she could always look through them just one more time.

She turned a page. "You're my hero. I'm *so* sick of moose."

They were all sick of moose by the end of winter. Moose soup, moose stew, moose potpie, mooseburger gravy on rice. Usually they would be getting more fresh meat and fish by this time, but everything was messed up in their house, and had been since Christmas.

Rigel wondered if she could go inside. She'd like to leave the hares for Lila and wash her hands with warm water and soap. She needed to clean the rifle. And she would have liked a little snack and a mug of tea. She was hungry after the long hours of walking, looking for hare tracks, kicking at scrub and waiting for startled hares to pop out from under the brush.

But the cabin door was closed.

"Yeah," Willow said; she must have seen where Rigel was looking. "Lila said to go play out for a while. Said she needed to talk to Bear."

Rigel and her sisters called their parents by their first names. They always had. It was one of their father's notions.

"Do you know what's going on?" Rigel asked.

"No clue, but Lila got another sat call this morning, so maybe it had something to do with that."

Their satellite phone was supposed to be reserved for business or emergencies. Its minutes cost a lot and it wasn't easy to charge either, given that they were off the grid and had no electricity. Until this past winter, Rigel had never seen her mom on the satellite phone for more than a minute or two, but lately Lila was taking it out into the cabin entryway, where she could have some privacy, and chatting on it for half an hour at a time.

"I'm *hungry*," Rigel grumbled, throwing herself down on the bench.

"I am too." Willow opened her magazine again. "Taylor Rocks Snapchat!" a headline shrieked in big pink letters. Who was Taylor? And what was Snapchat? Probably some TV show, Rigel guessed. If Willow were in a better mood, Rigel would have asked her, but she could tell by Willow's quick flipping of pages that she was nervous, and when Willow was nervous, she got cranky. Better leave her alone.

Rigel rested her back against the cabin wall and closed her eyes.

Rigel's folks had always fought now and then, but Rigel could remember when their arguments were about important things, like how many traplines to run or whether to buy a second snow machine. She wasn't sure when those arguments had gotten hotter and more frequent. It happened gradually, the way a full teakettle heats up until it's red-hot and whistling furiously. By last fall, Bear and Lila were fighting about anything. They could argue for two hours about how many rows of carrots to plant in the garden. The last, biggest, and dumbest argument had been on Christmas Eve, about whether to have blueberry pie or spice cake for Christmas dinner. Lila ended up making pie and Bear cake. The grown-ups did their baking without speaking, which wasn't easy in the cabin's tight quarters. On Christmas Day, they still weren't talking, and Rigel had made sure to have a slice of each dessert, to avoid taking sides.

A few days after Christmas was when Bear and Lila had sat the girls down and told them they'd decided a divorce was best, for everyone. That things between them weren't going to get better.

And a few overnight trips to Fairbanks was all it took. Rigel could hardly believe it was that simple, but there were the papers in Bear's old briefcase with the cardboard showing at its corners. *Dissolution of Marriage* was written right across the top.

Rigel hadn't minded much. That's what she'd told herself anyway. At least her parents wouldn't be shouting at each other anymore, or going through one of those times when they weren't speaking at all, which was almost worse than the yelling.

But the rest of the winter in their cabin was so strange it was almost as bad as the days when Bear and Lila were arguing all the time.

For one thing, there were the sleeping arrangements. In a two-room cabin, there weren't a lot of options. The girls had the cabin's smaller room, with its one window and three bunks. Bear and Lila slept in the main room, the bigger one. On one side was their big brass bed, the one Bear had ordered all the way from L.L.Bean in Maine and brought down from town in their skiff as a surprise for Lila. On that side of the cabin too was the old sofa covered with a balding caribou skin, shelves for tools and books and stuff, the pedal sewing machine, and the workbench. In the center of the room was the big table where Rigel's family ate and studied and did paperwork and played games, and then there was the kitchen area on the other wall, with the shelves and cupboards, woodstove, and wringer washer.

After Bear and Lila's divorce, Lila kept sleeping in the double bed and Bear had to make other arrangements. He tried sleeping on the floor, but it just got too cold there during the winter nights, and the sofa was too small, so he took to spreading out his sleeping bag on the cabin table. Rigel, who was always up first in the morning, could never get used to seeing Bear snoring gently in the spot where they were going to be eating breakfast an hour later.

All winter her parents were distracted. Not grouchy, or snappy. *Distracted*, like part of them was always somewhere else. They didn't plan the summer garden, or talk about spring hunting or fishing, or decide who was going to go away this year to do seasonal work and make some cash. Easter hadn't been much fun. There had been no Easter dinner or Easter egg hunt in the snow done with candy eggs, since they almost never had fresh ones. As for Rigel's birthday, Rigel suspected from the last-minute scramble that her parents had both almost forgotten.

From somewhere close came the steady thump of Izzy's jump rope.

Beside Rigel, Willow turned a page with a slithery rustle.

Rigel shifted restlessly on the bench.

At least she couldn't hear anyone yelling. That had to be a good thing.

In some of Rigel's library books, the books that Lila borrowed for them through the mail, kids' parents got divorced. In most of those stories, the parents divided up the furniture and cars and bank accounts, and one of them rented an apartment or a house, and the kids' lives carried on like they had before, as far as Rigel could tell, except for the divorce.

But Rigel and her family didn't live like the people in those books. They didn't have any cars or big bank accounts. Pretty much all they owned was this cabin on a creek off the Yukon River. They lived on what they could grow, hunt, and fish, and what they could afford to buy from the cash Bear and Lila scrounged up. Lots of people in the Bush lived the way they did: without running water, without indoor plumbing, without electrical wires, without regular jobs, without neighbors. Bush rats, people called them.

But that was going to be changing for either Bear or Lila, because one of them would have to move away now.

Maybe back to Fort McPhee, where Lila and Bear met and Willow and Rigel had lived when they were little. Maybe to Galena. Maybe even Fairbanks.

Would the girls move too, or would they be staying here?

That was what Bear would call the million-dollar question, the one that was making Rigel lose sleep and poke listlessly at her food. Anytime she made herself think about it, her heart started beating faster and her hands started to sweat—

The cabin door swung open.

"Come on in, girls," Lila called. "Your father and I need to talk to you."

Chapter 2

Inside, Bear stirred the fire in the woodstove, adding a few pieces of wood. The kettle was steaming, and Lila was getting down tea mugs.

Rigel left the pack in the entryway but hesitated over the gun. Her parents had taught her to clean her rifle first thing. Bear must have noticed, because he took the gun from her, did the usual checks quickly, and then put it up on the rack.

"I'll clean it later," he promised, and that's when Rigel knew something serious was about to happen.

"Did you get something?" Lila wanted to know.

"Two hares," Rigel said dully. This was her time to be patted on the back and congratulated, and she wasn't even looking forward to it now. But Bear and Lila did the best they could.

"Not bad!" Bear said, the way she knew he would.

"Nice job," Lila said. "How do you guys want them?" she teased. "Panfried, or casserole?"

"Casserole," everyone said at once.

This was an old joke in their family, and a year ago they all would have laughed. Today no one did, although Lila did her best to smile.

Lila was wearing her old red sweater, with her dark brown hair in a long braid over her shoulder. Her sleeves were shoved up and you could see the muscles in her lean arms move as she poured hot water into mugs. She brought over a plate of jam sandwiches, pushing it close to Rigel before sitting down.

Bear was a big man, and, sitting next to Lila, he seemed extra big. His thick blond hair was caught back in a bushy ponytail, and his golden beard reached the top of his coveralls.

It was Willow who asked, "What's going on, Lila?"

"What's going on," Lila said, "are some changes."

Rigel didn't like the sound of that, but Willow sounded excited when she asked, "Are we moving?"

Rigel remembered when Willow had loved the Bush, the same way Rigel and Izzy still did. And then Willow started changing. She got interested in those shiny fashion magazines you could get in the mail. She tore out pictures she liked and stuck them up on the wall by her bunk and mooned over good-looking village boys she'd only talked to a few times. Those crushes were pointless because they lived hours from town, either by boat or by snow machine, and only went every month or so, to pick up mail and supplies. And even Fort McPhee wasn't exactly a major city. It was just another little Native village on the Yukon. But Willow was tired of bush life. She wanted to live in town. Rigel knew that her big sister was hoping for Galena or Fairbanks. Maybe even Anchorage.

"We're going to Connecticut."

The three girls were wordless. Even Izzy, who usually chattered nonstop.

"Because Grandma's there," Lila explained. "We're going to be staying with her for a while. That'll give me a chance to get my feet on the ground and find a job and—well, figure out what to do next."

"Bailed out by Mom," Bear remarked to the air: not talking to Lila, not exactly.

"It's called a *loan*," Lila snapped. "And there's nothing wrong with it as long as we pay it back. Which we will."

He blew on his tea.

Rigel wrote Grandma every week. They all did. And Grandma wrote back, and sent clothes and presents, but Rigel had never actually met her. Willow had, once, before Rigel was born. Grandma had visited them in Fort McPhee. That was before Bear had inherited this place, his uncle's old hunting and fishing camp, before they'd moved downriver. Rigel had been a baby then.

Willow was excited, and Izzy was excited because Willow was excited. "Connecticut!" Izzy said, like it was Christmas.

Rigel didn't say anything. She didn't seem to be able to.

Lila said, "Rye, you know we can't stay here."

"Something's gotta give," Bear agreed.

Izzy scrunched up her forehead. "Lila, where is Connecticut?"

Lila went across to the bookshelf and brought back their old Rand McNally atlas. It was one of Rigel's favorite books. She'd spent many hours poring over it, looking at places she'd like to see one day. Mongolia and Borneo, Tibet and Greenland, places with more wilderness than town and more animals than people. Places like Alaska. The girls gathered around Lila as she opened the atlas to the big map of North America.

"Find Alaska for me, Izzy," Lila said.

Izzy found Alaska easily. Alaska hung up there in the northwest corner of the map off Canada, all by itself, too huge to be overlooked.

"Good girl. And we are going . . . here." Lila's finger traveled down through Alaska and then Canada and when it got to Washington State, Lila moved it across the country, away from the Pacific Ocean—through Idaho, Montana, Wyoming, North Dakota, Minnesota, Wisconsin, Michigan, Ohio, Pennsylvania, and New York—until at last her finger came to rest on a little pink rectangle beside the Atlantic Ocean.

Connecticut was in a jam-packed space up in the northeast corner of the Lower 48, where many little states were squashed in together. Rigel could cover three or four of them with just her thumb.

She'd never even bothered to examine that page in the atlas.

It was just a snarl of towns and roads—what Bear called "all that suburban crap."

Now Lila was explaining how they were going to take the boat to Galena, and then catch a small plane to Fairbanks, and then catch another flight that would go first to Seattle, Washington, and then all the way across the country to John F. Kennedy Airport in New York City—New York City!—where Grandma would meet them.

Rigel got up and went to the door. She had her hand on the doorknob when Lila said, "Where are you going, Rye Bear?"

"Just outside for a second." If she didn't get outside and take some deep breaths of fresh air, those jam sandwiches would be on their way back up.

"Take the wash water with you and throw it out, would you?" Lila said.

Rigel went to the counter and picked up the dishpan sloshing with gray water left from washing the breakfast dishes. Lila had saved it in case she decided to wash the floor. They packed their water up from the stream in buckets and they never wasted a drop.

Rigel carried it quickly into the entryway, kicking the door shut behind her, set the dishpan down on the bench, and steadied herself with a deep breath. The entryway had its own familiar smell that she'd always liked: damp clothes, wood smoke, and sweat, with a little fresh air and stinky feet thrown in, and underneath everything else, a faint tangy whiff of old muskrat.

She slowly put on her hoodie and boots and opened the outside door.

They threw out their dishwater far from the cabin. Used dishwater had a dank, discouraging smell. Even today, Rigel wouldn't dump the water out next to the cabin, like some slob who didn't care or didn't know any better. She carried the dishpan away from the house before she flung the water into the air, in one long sparkling sheet, and watched it splash into a thicket of willow. Holding on to the dishpan, Rigel walked down to the stream.

They lived up one of the little streams that fed into the Yukon River the same way the Yukon flowed west to feed into the Bering Sea. They took the battered aluminum skiff out onto the stream, splashed in its icy water on hot summer days, and fished from it. In the winter, the stream froze and became a wide white path through the scrub around their cabin. Frozen over, it was their highway—you could take a snow machine out onto it, follow it down to the river, and be at Fort McPhee or Galena in barely any time at all. Although you always had to be careful. Ice could be tricky. It could fool you, especially the overflow ice that could look safe and secure until the moment you went through it. And if you went through the ice on the river, and the current swept you downriver under more ice, you wouldn't be coming up again till spring.

That was the way Bear always put it to the girls, to make sure they remembered to be careful.

There were no roads where they lived. No house other than theirs for miles in every direction. Visitors came by snow machine or dogsled or boat. Hunters and fishermen occasionally, a few lost tourists, but mainly people they knew, people who went out of their way to stop in because they understood how hungry you could get for new faces living the way Rigel's family did.

Rigel turned restlessly back up toward the cabin. She didn't want to go in, where Lila was probably still talking about Connecticut. And she was almost always happier outside anyway.

The cabin door opened and Bear came out.

He walked down to where Rigel was standing, put his arm around her, and squeezed her tight against his side. His soft laughter floated out over her head.

"I told your mother you weren't going to be happy."

"What's it like in Connecticut?"

"Oh, honey. It's fake plastic crap top to bottom, like pretty much everything else down there."

By "down there," Bear meant the Lower 48. He sounded angry, the way he almost always did when he talked about life Outside.

"Have you been there?" Rigel asked.

"Not exactly," Bear admitted after a moment. "But that doesn't really matter, Rye Bear. Outside is pretty much the same wherever you go nowadays, thanks to TV." He pronounced the word "TV" with distaste, the way he always did. TV was one of Bear's things. Along with the Internet. Shopping malls. Public schools. Politicians. Interfering feds who showed up and poked their noses into people's private business, like how many moose they'd shot or where they were running their traplines. "I wanted you girls to grow up a different way, but your mother's made up her mind."

Something's gotta give.

Rigel hadn't done much traveling. Mostly back and forth to Fairbanks in small planes. She didn't like crowds. She knew that for sure. Even going to a dance at the Fort McPhee community center, where she knew lots of people, she had to take a deep breath outside and prepare herself to enter the crowded, noisy space. The Bush was where Rigel was happy. She never grumbled about eating moose for dinner again, or complained about the cold, or whined about hand-me-down clothes or shoes the way Willow sometimes did. Bear always said she did him proud. She thought again of the map Lila had shown them, of the little pink rectangle labeled Connecticut. Her heart started beating faster, and then Rigel got an idea.

An idea that made her feel like she'd thrown open a door and flooded a dark room with light.

"Bear, I'll just stay here. I'll just stay with you."

He shook his head and laughed. "I told her you would say that. I know you, Rye Bear. No one else in the world knows you the way I do."

Rigel felt a giddy burst of happiness and relief, like fireworks going off inside her.

"But no can do, kid."

The fireworks sputtered out, all at once.

"Because I'm going up to Prudhoe," Bear explained. "Soon as you girls are gone, I'm leaving too."

For extra money, Bear usually did firefighting. He had gone all over Alaska doing that, and even down to the Lower 48 once or twice. But he had worked up at Prudhoe too, in the big oil refineries on the North Slope. Firefighting jobs varied year to year, but there was always steady work on the pipeline.

He said, "I'm going to stick it out the whole year this time and put away a nice fat stash of dough."

Rigel swallowed. She tried to sound like an adult. "I could just stay in Fort McPhee with Kimora, then. Till you're back."

It was a good idea. She knew Sophie, Kimora's mom, would say it was okay, because Kimora had stayed with the Harmans once, back when Rigel and Kimora were both eight. Kimora's father had died that year and for a while after that Sophie was in bad shape. She couldn't even get out of bed in the morning. Kimora and her sister and brothers weren't getting to school and they weren't getting fed three times a day. So the kids went to stay with different people, until Sophie was doing better. Kimora came out to stay with the Harmans, and she was with them for almost a whole year. She did correspondence school with the girls, and helped with the chores, and slept in Rigel's bed, and that was when she had become Rigel's best friend.

Rigel had never had a friend outside the family before that.

Bear paused to think it over, then slowly shook his head. "Your mom isn't going to go along with that."

"Why?" Rigel tried to keep that "Why" short and business-like, but it came out wavering, dangerously close to whining.

"She wants you girls with her."

"We could ask her."

"Do me a favor and don't. Your mom's going to think I've been out here pouring poison into your ear."

Rigel's voice rose. "Then I'll just stay out here until you get back. I'll just stay here. I *won't* go to Connecticut."

That was a ridiculous idea, and she knew it even as she said it. An eleven-year-old girl living on her own in the Bush? Lila would never allow it. Even Bear wouldn't. And even if they agreed to such a crazy thing, other people never would. The moment anyone in Galena or Fort McPhee found out Rigel was wintering over alone, they'd be coming to collect her. No ifs, ands, or buts. And they would find out, because when it came to gossip, the Bush was worse than a church choir. Bear always said that.

She was headed for Connecticut.

She turned away from Bear so he couldn't see how scared she was, but he put his hands on her shoulders and gave her a little shake. His hands were big and hairy, and the left hand had a shiny pink scar where his forefinger should have been.

That finger had gotten caught in a winch on a fishing boat down in Bristol Bay.

Bear crouched down, peering into her face.

"Come on, Rye. You've got a good head, so use it. I'm only going to be on the Slope this one year. That's all. Then I'll be back with some money in my pocket and some options. Maybe I'll set up to be a guide. Or do boat tours on the river. Then when we talk to your mom about you coming back, it'll be a different story."

Rigel gave a long, shaky sigh. She wiped her nose with her sleeve, a habit her father hated, but he said nothing about her leaving a trail of snot on her clothes.

"Tell you what. We'll bring you back after school is over, next summer. So all you have to do is spend a year in Connecticut. Just one year! You keep your head down and go to school and do your chores and it'll be over before you know it. Remember, we named you after the best star in the whole night sky. What kind of star is Rigel again?"

"A blue supergiant."

"That's right. A blue supergiant star, the brightest one in the whole Orion constellation—that's you. And don't you forget it."

Rigel glanced up at the cabin. Lila was looking out one of the windows, checking on her. Rigel gave her nose another quick swipe, then raised her hand. Lila waved back and left the window.

"Lila won't let me come back," Rigel said.

"Now, come on. Your mom isn't going to stop you if she knows it's what you really want. And even if she tried, pretty soon you'll be at the age of informed consent. That means a judge will let you decide for yourself where you want to live."

Rigel sniffed. "You mean it?" As much as she loved Bear, she knew that his grand visions didn't always work out as planned.

Bear fished in his pocket. "Look."

It was a dog tag on a ball chain, like the dog tags Bear had worn in the Marines and kept in a box under the big bed. But this dog tag was made of silver and had a salmon engraved on one side, a jumping salmon with its tail curved over a fanning spray of water. It was beautiful, and it looked expensive.

"Got it for you for your birthday," Bear said. "But to be honest, things were so crazy in there I just plain forgot to give it to you."

"I knew it," Rigel muttered.

"Yeah, well, you take it now." Bear slipped the chain over her head and Rigel tucked the dog tag under her T-shirt. "Keep it hid, and whenever you're missing Alaska, you can look at this and know you'll be back in a year. Tops. It'll go quick, we'll both be so busy. Before you know it, we'll be back together, right here in the Bush, where we both belong."

Rigel pressed a hand to the front of her hoodie. Even through two layers of clothes, she could feel the solid rectangle of silver against her chest. It was a reassurance she could touch.

"But this plan stays between the two of us until I'm ready to talk to your mom about it. Understand, missy? No blabbing, no bragging. Especially not to your sisters. The last thing I need is a couple of hens clucking at me all winter about whether I've done this or thought about that. Got it?"

Rigel nodded.

Bear said, "That's my girl."

"But you have to promise," Rigel said.

He leaned over and pressed his nose to hers, the way he used to when she was little. "I promise."

Chapter 3

R igel."

Rigel kept her eyes squeezed shut.

"Rigel, I *know* you're awake." Willow poked her in the shoulder. "Come on, take a look—you'll miss it."

From the plane, New Jersey was covered with trees and looked like broccoli. The green bushy tops rolled away in every direction Rigel could see. Peeking through the trees were roofs of little houses, the occasional blue dot of a swimming pool, and clusters of bigger buildings surrounded by bald gray patches of parking lots. Roads threaded everywhere. Some were almost empty. Others were swarming with cars, which from high up looked like tiny but purposeful ants.

Willow had the window seat from Seattle to New York because Rigel had gotten the window seat from Fairbanks to Seattle.

Now New York City was coming up fast. The landscape changed slowly but steadily from green to gray. It was kind of like keeping an eye on a pot of oatmeal. The houses and buildings and roads thickened and clustered together and the green spaces got smaller and smaller, until finally there was a grayish porridge of rooftops and roads and parking lots passing underneath them, and the pilot was announcing their descent into New York.

Rigel couldn't help but feel a small twinge of excitement. Or maybe it was nervousness. Or both.

Well, at least from now on when Kimora bragged about trips to Anchorage, Rigel would be able to say, "*I've* been in New York."

Once the plane landed, there was the *snap-snap* of seat belts unfastening all around them, and the passengers sprang out of their seats and started rummaging for their bags in the overhead bins.

"Willow, Rye, just stay put," Lila called. "We'll take our time getting off."

Grandma was meeting them at baggage claim. Rigel was worried about finding it, even though Lila had said that there were signs all over the airport showing where it was. And Lila kept checking to make sure she still had Grandma's cell phone number. The number was on a piece of paper in Lila's wallet, and the paper was falling apart from Lila taking it out and checking it "just one more time."

That was how Rigel could tell that Lila was nervous too.

They were the last people to leave the plane.

"Buh-bye!" the flight attendants said.

"Have fun in New York!" one called to Izzy.

"I'm going to live in *Connecticut!*" Izzy said, loud and wild, the way she got when she was super tired.

The nice flight attendant said, "Well, that's exciting! Good luck!"

They stepped through the door into a long white tube that was kind of like something on the International Space Station, except that it had very dirty blue carpet and, at the far end, a crowd of frowning people waiting with their roll-on suitcases and boarding passes.

They'd finally arrived in New York City.

That morning they'd been in Fairbanks. Well, if anyone would call 1:30 a.m. "morning." It was more the middle of the night, even if it had been one of those strange, bright evenings of midsummer, when central Alaska stays light almost round the clock. And now they were in New York.

The crowd waiting to board seemed to be staring at them as they finally came out. Another crowd sat in the molded plastic chairs of the waiting area, and a third crowd of people tromped along the linoleum hallway between huge grimy sheets of glass that looked out onto the runways. Crowds everywhere.

The people pushed huge baby strollers. They yanked at wheeled bags. They stared into smartphones as they walked, or clamped them to their ears and talked loudly. Some people had earpieces and they looked like they were talking to themselves, like old folks did sometimes in Fort McPhee. But old folks in Fort McPhee muttered. They didn't conduct their one-sided conversations in bright loud voices.

I told you the boys have a baseball game tonight—

The doctor said I needed more exercise, so—

Well, just pick up a pizza, then!

Beep beep beep!

A cart whizzed past. A uniformed man drove it, and two old ladies sat at the very back, canes between their knees. The crowd parted before the cart and then swam back together again after the vehicle passed through, just like fish schooling in the river back home.

"There's the sign for baggage claim." Lila spoke softly, like she was talking to herself. "Okay, Lila. You can do this. Come on, girls."

Izzy held up her arms. She was too big to be carried, but Lila hoisted her up anyway. "This way." She started maneuvering through the crowds.

It was easy for Lila to say "This way," but there was someone in Rigel's path. Wherever she turned, someone was there. Willow was hesitating too. At least they would be lost together. Then Willow grabbed Rigel's hand and yanked her into the crowd. People glanced at them, just barely, and adjusted their pace so there was a place for them. That was how it worked. It really was just like the fish.

They hurried past shops selling clothes, books, magazines, postcards. Past vending machines and shoeshine stands. Past restaurants selling burgers, ice cream, cinnamon buns, coffee. Rigel caught delicious whiffs as they hurried past. She was hungry.

She had to pee too.

A big set of signs arched over the hallway ahead. And Rigel could see what was under the signs: the up and down escalators.

"*Lila!*" Rigel called.

None of them liked escalators. Not even Lila, who said she wasn't used to them anymore. But Rigel was the one who'd almost fallen down the escalator in the Seattle airport. Lila had promised she wouldn't make the girls try escalators again on this trip.

Lila finally slowed down. "Okay, okay. Over here."

It turned out there were old-fashioned, nonmoving stairs to one side. Rigel wasn't all that used to stairs either, but she could manage them. And the stairs were much less crowded. That was another bonus.

"What are escalators for?" Rigel asked Lila as they went downstairs.

"They're faster, and people don't have to use any energy to climb up and down them. They just get carried along." Lila boosted Izzy higher on her hip.

"But some people are walking on them," Willow pointed out.

It was true. Some people stood to the right, unmoving, and other people went around them so they could run down even faster. Rigel was sure if she ever tried that she would just fall again.

"Those are people in a bigger hurry," Lila said.

Late for their funerals. That's what Bear liked to say about people in a rush. Rigel pursed her lips the way he would have done. "What are they in such a hurry *for?*"

"Good question," Lila said, which was what grown-ups said when they didn't know the answer to something or didn't want to get into an explanation.

Someone bumped Rigel hard from behind and a girl about her own age squeezed past. She didn't look like any of the girls Rigel knew, with their hand-me-down clothes and hair that their mothers cut. Or even like the Fairbanks girls. This girl looked like a miniature adult, with perfect hair and an outfit that belonged on one of the models in Willow's magazines.

She didn't say "Excuse me." She didn't even glance over.

So this was what it was like Outside! People practically knocking someone else over and not even stopping to make sure they were okay.

It was going to be a long year.

"Rigel, you okay, babe?" Lila used her free hand to smooth down Rigel's hair.

Rigel shook off Lila's hand. "Escalators are stupid."

They had found out about Connecticut in May, and today was the first day of August. But Rigel still wasn't talking to Lila very much. She wasn't being dumb about it, the way Lila and Bear used to be, not exchanging a word for days on end and asking the girls to run messages like "Tell your father dinner is ready" or "Ask your mother where she put my chisel." That was awful for everyone. But she only talked to Lila when she had to.

"It's going to be fine," Lila said. "Look, there's our baggage claim. Now we'll—"

Sitting by the luggage carousel in one of the molded plastic chairs was a woman Rigel knew from photographs, a small, plump woman with short silver hair and red cat-eye glasses. The woman peered at them. Then she jumped out of her seat, her handbag falling to the floor.

"Lila!" Grandma said.

Lila put Izzy into Willow's arms and rushed to greet Grandma. They threw their arms around each other and rocked back and forth wordlessly for a long time, without letting go. Grandma finally took Lila by her shoulders and held her away to have a good look.

"Lila girl! Oh, I've missed you."

"It's been a long time. Too long, Mom."

Now it was the girls' turn, and Rigel braced herself against an unwanted hug. But Grandma didn't grab at them, or gush about how big they were, or do any of the other things Rigel had been dreading.

"Willow, I love your top," Grandma said. "Did you make that yourself? Rigel, I bought you a book of those math puzzles you like. It's waiting on your bed with a nice sharp pencil. You can start one the moment we get home, if you want. Hello, Izzy! Guess what I've got for dessert? Something special—cannoli."

They didn't know what cannoli were. Grandma explained that they were crunchy pastry tubes filled with sweet cream.

"These are from DiNapoli's. That's the best place close to us for cannoli. I stopped on the way down."

"DiNapoli's is still there?" Lila asked. "Mr. DiNapoli can't be running it anymore, can he?"

"He only comes in now and then—his son runs it now. You girls sit down. You must be exhausted. Your mom and I will get the luggage."

At the mention of the luggage, Izzy gave a whimper.

"Come on, Izzy," Rigel said. "Be a big girl now."

All of them had had to leave stuff behind in Alaska, important stuff they cared about. Lila had been strict about the baggage, because extra baggage cost money to ship. They'd each been allowed two garbage bags for the plane to Fairbanks, and then Lila bought them each a duffel bag there, because you couldn't take garbage-bag luggage onto a jet plane going Outside.

The garbage bags were supposed to be full of clothes, but Willow had smuggled a few of her favorite magazines. Rigel had hidden a bag of salmon jerky. And Izzy had brought her jump rope. Its plastic handles had been repaired with silver duct tape, and according to Izzy, those silver handles gave this jump rope special powers.

Besides their garbage-bag essentials, they'd been allowed to mail themselves three boxes each to Grandma's address in Connecticut. But even those boxes couldn't be too heavy, Lila said, or they would cost too much to ship.

That was all they could bring with them.

At the luggage carousel, Lila wrestled the last bulging duffel onto their cart.

Grandma came back over. "Now, who needs to use the bathroom?" she asked, much to Rigel's relief. She'd had to go forever.

It was great to pee at last, but the roar of the bathroom hand dryers was so awful even Willow didn't want to linger in front of the big mirrors. (And Willow used the mirror in their cabin so much Bear made jokes about her wearing it out.) In just a few minutes, they were back out in the baggage claim area, wiping their wet hands on their pants.

"Okay, I'll push the cart," Lila said. "Izzy, Grandma is going to hold your hand. Willow, you keep an eye on Rigel."

"I don't need anyone to keep an eye on me," Rigel protested, insulted, but the adults acted like she hadn't said anything.

"You heard her." Willow stood a little straighter, the way she did when she was trying to look grown-up.

Outside, it was crowded again, even more crowded than

the hallways in the airport. And louder too. Noisy planes. Zooming cars. People shouting to one another, or shouting into their phones. Brakes squealing as big buses pulled in and burped their exhaust over the people on the sidewalks.

But the worst was the honking. Every tap was like a nail banging into Rigel's head. She couldn't relax. Every time she would finally manage to take a deep breath, there would be another loud *blaaaaaaaat!* just beside her, and she would jump.

"Make sure you obey the traffic lights," Grandma said. "Even when you see the walking man, *look* before you step off the curb. Do you hear me, girls? Every single time."

Rigel wiped her damp hands on her jeans again.

Anyone would get nervous hearing a speech like that.

But they crossed with no trouble. And the other side of the road was much less crowded. Rigel could breathe easier right away.

They walked through the dim parking lot to a big white minivan. Its doors unlocked with a click from Grandma's key and the side door slid open by itself, without anyone having to touch it.

"I rented it for the day," Grandma said to Lila.

The van was like a house on wheels. Rigel knew of cabins that were smaller.

They stowed their luggage in the back, and Willow and Rigel sat in the second row of seats with Izzy between them. There was a strong piney smell that made them all sneeze. Lila took down the little cardboard tree hanging from the rearview mirror and put it in the glove compartment.

"Seat belts please. All right. Here we go." Grandma started to back out and then stopped short as a car zoomed by, honking savagely. "Now, remind me. Did you guys have a car?"

"We never did." Lila shrugged. "Not even in Fort McPhee. The roads didn't go anywhere once you were out of town. A snow machine was more practical."

"But we've *ridden* in plenty of cars," Willow added.

And they had, although Rigel was more used to boats and snow machines and ATVs. She liked them better too.

Grandma drove out of the parking lot and merged onto the highway.

They hurtled along the narrow road with only a concrete barrier separating them from the cars pouring in the other direction. If Rigel had rolled down her window and reached out, she could have touched that barrier. And if Willow had rolled down her window, she could have touched the hand of someone in the next car, not that anyone was looking over at them. They were all acting like this driving thing was no big deal. Grandma took it casually too. She was chatting to Lila as she drove, laughing, calling questions into the backseat. If Rigel had known her grandma better, she would have reminded her to be careful. As it was, she clutched her seat belt and hoped for the best.

An orange detour sign loomed ahead, and Grandma

squeezed their van over to the left into a lane that was already so crowded with cars and trucks Rigel didn't see how they could fit. It was like getting toothpaste back into a full tube. But Grandma managed it.

Rigel had never seen so much concrete. Gray pavement. Gray walls. Gray buildings. When she looked up at the sky, which was a trick she used in crowded towns, she couldn't even see it. At least not the sky Rigel was familiar with, with clouds and blue spaces. Here there was a flat brown haze overhead, the layer of exhaust from thousands of cars.

Rigel's heart started to beat faster. She closed her eyes and took a big calming breath.

"Grandma," she asked. "Are we close to Baldwin yet?"

Baldwin was the town where Grandma lived, their new home.

Rigel's *temporary* home.

But that was a secret.

Her grandma glanced over her shoulder. "Oh, no. We've got another hour to go, at least."

That was good. She sank back, relieved.

Willow whispered urgently, "Rigel."

Willow nodded at Izzy, who sat hunched between the two of them, her face white and slick with sweat. For once Izzy didn't dare open her mouth to speak, because it wasn't words that were going to come out.

Willow punched the buttons on her armrest. She stabbed at one, then another, obviously trying to get the window down—there were so many buttons!—but they didn't have that much time.

Up front, between the bucket seats with Lila and Grandma, there was a big plastic bag. Rigel snatched it up. Something heavy bumped in the bottom, but she ignored that and fumbled the bag open under Izzy's chin just in time. Izzy leaned forward and a whole day's worth of airport food poured out into the bag in long slimy strands. Vomit spaghetti.

The gross smell filled the car. Lila turned around to stare at the backseat, and Grandma was peering into the rearview mirror.

Lila said softly, "That was the bag with the cannoli in it."

Chapter 4

I'm sorry," Izzy whispered.

"It happens, sweetie," Lila said. "Do you think you're okay now?"

Izzy nodded, wiping her mouth. Rigel could tell she was too embarrassed to say anything more.

Grandma said, "Good thinking back there. I'd rather have a bagful of puke than a carful of puke, any day."

Rigel decided right then that she liked Grandma.

She didn't like New York, and maybe she wasn't going to like anything about Connecticut either, but she definitely liked Grandma.

Grandma snapped on the turn signal. "Lila, do you

remember the time your brother ate too many lobster rolls in Maine?"

"Dad *warned* him three was too many—" There was laughter bubbling up in Lila's voice.

"But he could hardly talk, when he'd had three himself. Well, girls, your uncle Vance turned green outside of Kennebunk and all of a sudden he rolled his window down as fast as he could and stuck his head outside—"

Lila had her arms folded across her stomach, she was laughing so hard. "It's the only time Dad ever had the car washed on a vacation!"

"You see, Izzy, you're not the only one. It's a family tradition," Grandma finished. "Now, there's a gas station up there— Let me pull over."

They threw the cannoli bag away, and even though the sign inside said NO PUBLIC RESTROOM, the lady behind the counter let them use the bathroom. Izzy got cleaned up, and Grandma bought everyone a can of ginger ale and told them to sip the cold drinks slowly. Then they got on the road again.

"I wish I knew somewhere on the way home where we could stop for more cannoli," Grandma mused. "DiNapoli's will be closed by the time we're anywhere close. The only place I can think of right now is Veniero's, but that's in Manhattan—"

"Mom, we should probably just head home. I'm exhausted, and you know what the traffic will be like."

"Lila," Willow protested. Rigel could tell she was wild to get up close and personal with Manhattan.

Lila said, "Willow, listen, I'll take you into the city next week. We'll have lunch and go to a few museums. We can catch the train from Stamford."

"Really?!" Willow breathed, and Lila said yes, they should have time to do that before she found a job and started working again.

"You girls can come too," Lila said to Izzy and Rigel.

Izzy perked up. No one would ever think she'd just finished hurling everything down to her toenails. But Rigel summoned her best shrug. Like going into Manhattan would be the most boring thing in the world.

"Well, I don't want to," she said. "And Izzy will probably just get sick on the train, so I'd bring a bag along if I were you."

Her little sister deflated like an old balloon.

"Are you sure?" Grandma asked. "There are a lot of wonderful museums in the city. The Museum of Natural History has a room with a ninety-four-foot blue whale hanging from the ceiling."

It took Rigel a moment to think of a comeback to this.

"Is it a *real* whale?" she demanded.

"Rigel." Lila's calm voice carried a warning. "Of course it's not real. It's a fiberglass model."

"Well, I've seen real whales, so I don't need to look at fake ones."

Willow pushed her hair back. "If you're talking about Utqiagvik, I call bullcrap on that. You were only three. You don't even remember that trip."

"I do too remember!" Rigel snapped.

She couldn't remember everything, but she remembered a lot. She remembered the huge bowhead whale on the beach, surrounded by busy, excited people. People were always excited after a successful hunt. She remembered the whale's huge mouth that stretched halfway along its body and made it look like it was smiling. She'd felt sad it was dead, she remembered that too. And some grown-up who leaned over to tease her, saying, "Yum yum yum!" and poking at her stomach.

Bear's tickly beard when he picked her up and kissed her . . .

The smell of the fur ruff on Lila's parka . . .

The taste of the *maktak* someone gave her, one of the pieces of whale skin and blubber the women prepared and passed around to celebrate.

"I do so remember. I remember the *maktak*," she said.

Willow clicked her tongue. "Yeah, right."

Rigel desperately wanted to tell Willow to shut up, but Lila's rule went that if anyone said "Shut up," that person had to pay everyone else in the room a dollar, and that got expensive fast.

"Manhattan is right over there and you girls are missing it," Lila remarked.

Willow pressed her nose to the window.

To the west, Manhattan's towers reached into the sky.

Willow pressed her nose to the window. "Oooh, that's the Chrysler Building, isn't it, Grandma? And that's the Empire State Building! Rigel, Izzy, look! That building is one hundred and two stories high!"

Izzy leaned across to get a better look. "They must have lots and lots of escalators."

That made Grandma and Lila laugh. Grown-ups always thought Izzy was cute.

"Turn around and see if you can spot the Freedom Tower farther south," Grandma suggested. "That's even higher than the Empire State."

The skyscrapers looked like big fangs. There was nowhere Rigel could rest her eyes, nowhere empty. She was so dizzy she had to cover her eyes with her hand.

That was better. She leaned her head against the door.

"Rye, are you all right?" she heard Lila ask.

"Find her a bag," Willow said.

Rigel swallowed hard. "It's okay. I'm just resting."

365 days. That's all she needed to survive.

52 weeks. About 9,000 hours. How many hours exactly? Rigel relaxed as she started the math in her head.

350 x 24 made 8,400—

10 x 24 made 240—that one was easy—

5 x 24 was the same as 10 x 12 and 10 x 12 made 120—another easy one—

—add them all up and get the answer—

That was how Rigel did math in her head, with all kinds of weird tricks and lazy shortcuts. She was the only person she knew who did it that way, but Bear and Lila said it was fine because it worked for her.

8,760. And she'd be asleep for a third of it, about 3,000 hours. She went to the bother of figuring it out exactly. 2,891 (if you rounded up). That left 5,869 waking hours to tolerate.

She sank down into the math like it was a warm sudsy bath. Math was the same whether she was in Alaska or in New York.

If she went to school for six hours a day, five days a week ($6 \times 5 = 30$) for nine months (call it 36 weeks), that made 1,080 hours in school. That was all? That was nothing. She was barely going to be in school at all.

But how many *minutes* was that . . . ?

‖‖‖

When Rigel woke up, her neck was stiff, and there was a spot on the front of her T-shirt where she'd drooled. Willow was sleeping with her head against the van window, her hair blazing brightly in the afternoon sunlight. Izzy slumped all the way over against Willow with her mouth wide open, the way she slept when she was out cold.

"First off you're going to need a cell phone," Grandma was saying.

Lila groaned. She sounded just like Willow.

"No arguments. You have to have one nowadays. And we'll update your résumé."

"I wish I knew what we were going to put on it." Lila sounded tense, and that made Rigel's stomach hurt. "I haven't had a day job in fourteen years."

"Honey, you haven't even been here a day. Relax. You can start worrying tomorrow."

"Mom. Thank you again for taking us in. If it weren't for you, I don't know what we would have done."

"Oh, I'm happy to have the company. You wouldn't believe how bored I've gotten since I retired. Besides, this means I'll have a chance to really get to know the girls."

"They're good girls," Lila said. "Raising them is the one thing I did right."

"Nonsense." Grandma sounded brisk. "You wanted to try bush life, and you gave it your best shot. So it didn't work out the way you hoped it would—that doesn't mean it was a mistake."

Mistake? How could anyone think their life in Alaska was any kind of mistake?

A life of concrete, and noise, and people everywhere—*this* place was the mistake.

"Where are we?" Willow asked sleepily.

Izzy stirred and rubbed her nose.

Grandma said, "We're in Connecticut. We're almost home."

The highway was much less crowded now. On each side of the road, trees rose up, huge trees with thin fluttering leaves that turned a bright green wherever the sunlight came through. Under them, grass rolled down to the roadside. This road was not lined with strip malls or billboards or buildings shoved in side by side. Just a few houses showing here and there through the woods. The tightness in Rigel's chest relaxed.

"This is our exit," Grandma said, swinging the car off the highway onto a narrower road.

Grandma turned off this road onto a smaller one, and then a smaller one yet. The car was quiet as they all peered out. It was kind of like boating up the Yukon to their own nameless stream.

Willow yelped and pointed to a sign saying WELCOME TO BALDWIN, CONNECTICUT. ESTABLISHED 1750.

This was it. How many letters had Rigel addressed to Baldwin, CT?

They drove through an old-fashioned downtown with striped awnings and trees lining the sidewalks.

"There's a nail salon," Willow said. "There's an ice cream parlor. And there's a stationery store—"

"What's that?" Izzy wanted to know, but Willow went right on.

"A Mexican restaurant—a bakery—a bank—another bank—toy store—look, a movie theater!"

Then they were leaving the downtown and coming into a neighborhood filled with houses. They seemed enormous. Most of them were two stories and some were three. Some were painted, others were red brick, and one was made of big gray stones. There was not one house made of siding, or unpainted boards, or logs. And the houses were surrounded by green lawns, not hard-packed dirt clearings. There was almost no clutter. No rusty fifty-five-gallon drums, no broken-down snow machines waiting to be fixed, no dusty rolls of Visqueen or stacks of warping plywood, no sled dogs staked out and barking at everything going by . . .

Willow gasped. "Grandma, this is beautiful."

"Oh, this is a fancy part of town." Grandma sounded cheerful. "I'm afraid our house isn't anything like this grand."

It was true that the houses gradually shrank as they drove away from downtown. Still, they were all painted, they all had lawns and shrubs and trees, and some of them had gardens too. Grandma waited at a stoplight, then turned left. Rigel stared at the school on the corner, a large redbrick building with stone trim.

"That's where you're going to school, Izzy," Grandma said. "Nathan Hale Elementary. That's where your mom and uncle Vance went. This is our street."

Izzy leaned across Rigel's lap to get a better look.

That school building was *big*. You could have fit the entire population of Fort McPhee inside, and had room for more.

And the middle school, where Rigel would be going, would be even bigger than this one.

Rigel started to sweat. She pressed the dog tag under her shirt against her heart and could feel herself slow down and get calm again.

Just one year. That was all. 8,760 hours.

At least the houses on this street weren't so large, weren't like mansions. Where was Grandma's house, though? They rattled over a railroad crossing, and then Grandma slowed the car and turned into the driveway of a two-story house next to the tracks. Grandma's key fob chirped, and the back door of the van rolled open quietly.

Grandma's house was painted golden-yellow with green shutters and a glossy green front door. There was a separate garage, like an extra little house, at the end of the driveway, painted the same colors. It had two small cars parked inside.

"That's Vance's car." Grandma tapped the top of the red one. "And he said you were welcome to use it while he's gone."

Uncle Vance was spending a year in Antarctica, doing research on dark matter. Rigel knew all about his trip. She had to write him every week too.

The house's backyard had three of those towering trees Rigel liked, with smaller trees and bushes sprawled underneath, and the sunny front yard was full of flowers and shrubs. There was a big fenced vegetable garden on the side closest to the railroad tracks. Sunflowers leaned over the fence, and Rigel could smell tomato and basil plants.

Lila stood studying the house the way Rigel had, like she'd never seen it before. "It's just the same."

Grandma put her hand on Lila's shoulder. "The same little old house. But we'll all fit."

Grandma's house *was* one of the smallest on the block. But to Rigel it was big. It was hard to believe Grandma had been living here all alone for the years since Grandpa died.

Rigel walked over to the railroad tracks. They weren't fenced in. On either side of them, there was wasteland left to go wild. Trees, bushes, beds of fallen leaves, tangles of undergrowth. The wasteland was about as wide as Grandma's yard front to back, and it ran up and down the track in both directions. It was a little wilderness that ran through the roads and houses, like a vein through a leaf.

Chapter 5

N ow, girls," Grandma said, "the front door is for visitors. We use the side door. Right this way."

On the garage side of the house were concrete steps leading up to a second door. It must be a big house to need two doors.

Grandma bent over to slip off her sandals and they all followed suit.

"Just drop the bags right here and we'll take them upstairs later. Let me show you around."

They were in the dining room. There was a mat by the side door and hooks on the wall and a bench there, for people's dirty shoes and umbrellas and wet coats. That was familiar, like the entryway back home. But the empty dining room table, standing on a big colorful rug, was less familiar. Back in Alaska, their table was always crowded. Every mealtime they cleared things away to make room for the pots and plates. There was nothing on this table but a fancy glass bowl, carefully centered.

An old upright piano stood against one wall and on another was a big cupboard with glass doors to show off the plates and glasses inside. The plates were fancy, with rims of dark blue and gold. Rigel hoped Izzy would be careful when it was her turn to wash up.

A door led from the dining room into the kitchen at the back of the house. Willow opened the refrigerator door and let the cold air inside blow onto her face. Izzy went straight to the sink and started playing with the faucet. On and off, on and off.

"Iris!" Rigel said, scandalized. "Stop wasting water."

Izzy didn't even turn her head. "You're not the boss of me."

"Yeah, chill." Willow always stuck up for Izzy. "It's not her fault you're so stressed out lately."

"Izzy, you count to five and then turn that water off," Lila said. "It's wasteful. And Grandma pays for that water. It isn't free."

Izzy turned off the tap immediately. She understood about not wasting money. They all did. She ran over to a cupboard and opened it. Rigel had a brief glimpse of boxes and cans of food inside—at least that was familiar—before Izzy slammed the cupboard shut and flew over to another cupboard and opened it. This cupboard was full of dishes.

Wait a minute. The cupboard in the dining room was full of plates. How many dishes did Grandma have?

Rigel went back to the door to make sure she wasn't wrong about dishes in the dining room.

Grandma followed her. "That's the good china. We only use that on special occasions."

So the kitchen had its own dishes. And its own table too. This table was well used and well scrubbed, more like the one back home in their cabin. It was already set for dinner. The kitchen plates were sturdy and plain—more likely to stand up to Izzy's dishwashing. Still, how many sets of dishes did anyone need?

Her sisters were out of the kitchen already.

"Rigel, hurry up!" Izzy shouted.

Rigel peeked into the living room, a big room with slouchy furniture and lots of books. There was a stereo turntable with vinyl records scattered around it and a white-brick fireplace that smelled of wood smoke. But no sisters. She opened a hallway door and admired a little bathroom tucked under the stairs. Still no sisters. The next door opened to a coat closet.

The third door off the hallway popped open and Izzy's flushed face appeared.

"Come *on!*" she said. "There's a TV!"

Narrow stairs led down and Rigel followed Izzy carefully, gripping the banister.

There was another living room in Grandma's basement. It had narrow windows right up against the ceiling, and stained gray carpet, and apparently existed just as a place to watch TV, because the old brown-plaid sofa and a plush, cushioned armchair were set right in front of it.

"That's your grandfather's recliner," Grandma remarked.

"He lived in this thing," Lila said, giving it an affectionate pat.

Izzy scrambled into the chair. Then she pulled a wooden handle on the chair's side, and a footrest sprang up. When Izzy threw herself backward, the chair reclined.

If they'd had something like that in their cabin, Bear could have slept there last winter instead of on the table.

Izzy sat back up. "How long has Grandpa been dead?"

"Izzy," Willow hissed.

"It's okay, Willow," Grandma said. "Twelve years, Izzy, and I still miss him terribly. Your grandfather was a character. Smart, and stubborn . . ."

Lila said, "Wait until you get to know Rigel better. She's so much like Dad it's not even funny."

Rigel ignored this. She took after Bear. Everyone knew that, or should know it.

Izzy grabbed the remote and turned on the TV.

"Honey, turn that off," Lila ordered.

"But I want to waaaatch it! Lilaaaaaaaa—"

"Rigel," Willow called from a little hallway.

Willow had found a washer and dryer. That meant the laundry was going to be no trouble at all. Rigel knew that because there was a laundromat in Fort McPhee.

There was also another sink and toilet. How many bathrooms did people Outside need?

"I can't believe Grandma lived here alone," Willow whispered.

Rigel had been thinking the same thing.

"Do you think she used a different bathroom every day?" Rigel whispered back. "That's what I would do."

"Grandma," Willow called. Was she was going to quiz Grandma about her bathroom usage? Instead Willow asked, "How many bathrooms do you have?"

"Come upstairs and see," Grandma said. Which was clever of Grandma, because as soon as she said it, the TV was off again and there was a *bump-bump-bump-thump* on the stairs.

Izzy cried, "Owie!"

"Izzy, be careful!" came Lila's voice. "Go slower until you're more used to the stairs!"

But Rigel could tell there was no slowing Izzy down. She led their way out of the basement and up to the second floor.

At the top of the stairs was Grandma's room, which was the largest bedroom, with its own bathroom for Grandma's sole personal use. And they still weren't done with the bathrooms. There was another in the hall, with both a shower and a big old-fashioned bathtub.

"I'm afraid you'll have to share this one," Grandma said.

"Grandma, we didn't even *have* an indoor bathroom in Alaska," Willow reminded her.

"Are these all the bathrooms?" Rigel wanted to know.

Something about this struck everyone else as funny.

"Why?" Willow said. "Are you worried whether we have enough bathrooms, Rigel?"

That wasn't what Rigel had meant: she just wanted to confirm how many bathrooms the house had.

"This is the last one," Grandma said.

The house had four bathrooms, for the five of them.

Next to Grandma's bedroom was Uncle Vance's old room, which was going to be Lila's. The bedroom across the hall from Grandma's was going to be Willow's. Willow was getting that whole room to herself. And next door to Willow was Rigel and Izzy's bedroom.

"You're going to have to share," Grandma apologized again. "But it's a nice big room."

It was bigger than their old room, and all three of them had shared that. And Grandma had put two low bookshelves down the center of the room to divide it. One bookshelf faced right and one faced left, and both of them already had books in them. More books, on top of all those books downstairs.

"Some of those were your mom's and uncle's," Grandma said. "And lots of garage sale specials. Now, who wants a snack before we start unpacking?"

While everyone else went clattering back downstairs, Rigel stayed behind to catch her breath.

She shoved the puzzle book and pencil aside and sat on her own bed. She and Izzy weren't going to have to share a bed. They weren't going to have to share anything. They each had their own bed, chest of drawers, and table and chair. They even each had their own closet. They were in "the lap of luxury," as Bear would have called it.

Rigel knew what Bear would have to say about this house. There were plenty of big houses in Alaska. There were big cabins all over the Bush, mostly weekend places for people who didn't live there full-time. When Bear got out of the Marines, he'd had a job caretaking weekend cabins, buying groceries and filling water barrels and keeping the woodpiles high. Even arranging a fire ready to go in the woodstove so that all those lazy weekenders had to do was light a match. And some of them couldn't even do *that*, Bear would say.

He'd go on. "People like that should get their butts back to the Lower 48, and live the soft life down there if they want it that bad. Leave Alaska for the real bush rats, like us."

And he'd put his hand affectionately on Rigel's shoulder.

Bear didn't like those houses, and Bear wouldn't like this house either if he could see it.

"Only *four* bathrooms?" Rigel could imagine Bear saying. "Izzy doesn't get a bathroom of her own? Well, that's outrageous!"

Usually Rigel laughed herself sick at Bear's comments about spoiled city people. But now she actually knew one of them: Grandma. And Rigel could tell already that Grandma was a good person, even if she did have four bathrooms and two living rooms and two sets of dishes.

And, looking around this comfortable bedroom, she could already see the advantages to the soft life.

Rigel pressed her hand to her chest so she could feel the dog tag under her shirt.

卌

Dinner was mostly delicious. The vegetables had all come from Grandma's garden. Everything fresh, not one thing from a can. There was zucchini fried with garlic and basil, and a tomato and mozzarella salad. The milk was fresh too, not mixed up from powder.

"Is the salmon good?" Grandma asked. "Your mom said you girls liked it."

So *that's* what this fish was supposed to be. It was a weird grayish pink, instead of orangey-red, with thick layers of bitter gray fat.

"It's fine," Willow said politely, washing the salmon down with milk.

"The man at the fish store assured me this was wild salmon," Grandma said, watching them.

"Was he sure?" Izzy said, poking at it.

"Girls. Eat your fish," Lila said.

"May I be excused for a second?" Rigel asked Lila.

She could tell by her mom's raised eyebrows that Lila thought she was trying to get out of eating the salmon. She tried again. "Please?"

"Come right back," Lila said.

Rigel ran up to her room—she was already getting used to the stairs—and was back down in a minute with a ziplock bag full of glistening red sticks of fish.

"Salmon strips!" Izzy shouted.

"Is this what you bring to Connecticut instead of underwear and socks?" Lila's smile gave away that the stern tone was only pretend.

Rigel doled out a piece for each of them.

"This is Rigel's favorite food in the whole world," Willow said to Grandma.

The salmon jerky tasted like Alaska—it was smoky, and salty, and sweet. Because salmon jerky was good trail food, light and satisfying, it was the taste of long days out on the land, hunting or fishing, checking traplines, gathering berries. Or just having fun.

"I can see why." Grandma chewed with her eyes half-closed. "Such a rich flavor."

Rigel's piece was already done. She would have liked another one, but this bagful needed to last her a while. Maybe Bear would send more. She knew Lila's gaze was on her, so she picked up her fork and finished the store-bought salmon on her plate. It didn't taste like salmon to her. It didn't taste like much of anything.

"We don't have cannoli," Grandma said, once the salmon was all eaten, "but there's some ice cream. Just vanilla, I'm afraid."

"Ice cream, yum," Izzy said.

"You girls seem pretty excited about plain old vanilla ice cream." Grandma glanced teasingly at Lila. "Your mom would have asked where the chocolate syrup was."

"Mom," Lila said with the faintest edge of exasperation in her voice. "You always forget we didn't have a fridge or a freezer out at our place. The girls didn't get ice cream very often."

"Or fresh zucchini and tomatoes," Willow said.

Or garlic, Rigel added to herself. The garlic had tasted especially good, because they had never had any luck growing it and that meant they didn't get it very often. "We had plenty of snow ice cream, though," she said, defending bush life the way she always did.

"Snow ice cream?" Grandma asked.

"You can make it when there's fresh snow. You just mix the snow with some sugar and chocolate syrup."

"That sounds excellent." Grandma leaned back in her chair and put an elbow over the back, the same way Lila always did. "You need to make some for me as soon as we have snow on the ground."

Lila put a bowl of ice cream in front of Rigel. She dug her spoon into the ice cream and closed her eyes as its cold creaminess dissolved in her mouth. It was smoother and richer than snow ice cream. It tasted good. Almost annoyingly good.

After dessert, the girls did the dishes. But with the big

sinks and running hot water and bright kitchen lights, it didn't even feel like work.

✝✝✝

That night, Izzy and Rigel's bedroom was quiet and empty with only the two of them in it. Even though Rigel was bone-tired from the long day, it took her a while to fall asleep and she woke up only a few hours later, feeling hot. Someone had put a flannel blanket over her, and she kicked it down with her feet. Izzy's peaceful breath sawed in and out. Something else was sawing too. There was a weird noise coming from outside, kind of a rhythmic creaking, but loud.

Creak creak creak. Creak creak creak.

Rigel got up and pulled aside the curtain.

The sun had set hours ago—weirdly quickly, like a bright basketball sinking below the horizon instead of bouncing along it for a while, the way it did on the Yukon in midsummer. But even though the sun was gone, the sky wasn't dark. It was a strange dirty orange instead, like the sponge she'd used on the dinner dishes, and she could barely see any stars.

Creak creak creak, creak creak creak.

The door squeaked and Willow came in, barefoot in her nightshirt, with a pillow under her arm.

"What is that noise?" Willow whispered.

"An alarm?" Rigel guessed.

"Girls." Another whisper from behind them. Lila. "What are you doing?"

"What's that sound?" Willow asked, for both of them.

"It's crickets," Lila said. A smile twitched at her mouth, but Rigel could tell her mom was too tired to laugh.

How could a tiny insect make a noise that huge? "Are they going to be doing that every night?" Rigel demanded.

"Every night while it's warm, but in another few days you won't even hear it unless you listen for it. Now, it's after midnight—"

"I don't like the sky, either," Rigel went on. "Look out there. It's orange."

"Rigel Jane—" Lila pinched her nose and squeezed her eyes shut. The crickets shrieked outside. She said at last, "Look, we're all tired. You two get in bed and go to sleep and don't you dare wake up your sister." She closed the door quietly on her way out.

"You didn't have to be obnoxious," Willow whispered.

"Me?!" Rigel whispered back.

Willow didn't even bother to answer, just got into Rigel's bed and wiggled down comfortably. There was plenty of room, as long as neither of them was a bed hog.

"It was weird in there by myself," Willow murmured.

"It's all weird here," Rigel said.

"I guess we'll get used to it." Willow punched up her pillow and turned over.

Rigel lay on her back, staring at the ceiling.

Creak creak creak, creak creak creak.

She had no intention of getting used to any of this. Not that gross sponge-colored sky. And especially not those stupid crickets. Because what cranky Lila and bossy Willow didn't know was that next summer, when these crickets were starting up their racket again, Rigel would be gone.

Chapter 6

Is that what you're wearing, your first day of school?" Willow put down her lip gloss and kissed at the air.

Rigel dropped her spoon into her bowl of oatmeal and groaned.

"Rye Bear, try to get something in your stomach." Lila sliced banana onto Izzy's cereal. "Willow, you need to stop."

"I laid out an outfit for you," Willow continued.

"It had a skirt." Rigel didn't like skirts. They made her feel conspicuous. She was wearing her favorite pair of jeans and her Tanana Valley State Fair T-shirt.

"And do you have to wear your hair in those braids?" Willow went on. "You look like someone out of *Little House on the Prairie*."

"Rigel looks fine," Lila said.

"Okay." Willow shrugged. "If she wants to look like she just doesn't care, on the first day of school, whatever."

Willow wore a blue dress with white embroidery, new from the mall. Her bright golden hair was combed out and hanging loose, the way she always wore it now: it hung all the way to her waist.

"At least tell me you didn't pack a sardine sandwich," she said.

Rigel froze with her mug halfway to her mouth.

"*Rigel! No* sardines. I can't believe you even thought of those. They *stink*. And no Spam either," Willow went on, ruling out Rigel's second-favorite sandwich.

"What am I supposed to eat?"

"There's some turkey in the refrigerator. Have that."

Rigel crammed a piece of bacon into her mouth. This was it for breakfast. She was way too nervous to eat anything else. She went to the counter, slapped together a new sandwich, and stuffed it into her lunch box.

"And be careful where you sit at lunch," Willow said from behind her. "Try to make sure you sit with the right kids. The popular ones. If you don't know what to say, just smile a lot and laugh at everyone's jokes. And you can always ask people questions about themselves."

"Willow, enough," Lila said. "You're making your sister more nervous, not less."

"*I'm* not nervous." Izzy smiled, slurping at her juice.

"Good for you," Rigel muttered.

"Lila, have you seen my phone?" Grandma called down from upstairs. "I can't find it anywhere, and I wanted to take some pictures before the girls leave for school."

"I think I saw it in the basement, Mom. I'll check."

The moment Lila was out of the kitchen, Rigel gathered her dishes, put them in the sink, and grabbed her lunch.

She hated the kind of pictures where she had to stand smiling while someone chirped, "Say cheese!" And she didn't want another argument about whether someone needed to walk her to school the first day. Or whether she should try just one more bite of oatmeal.

She was in the dining room with her hand on the doorknob when Willow said, "Stop right there."

"Make me," Rigel said.

"You let me fix your hair, or I'm calling Lila right now." Willow put her hands on her hips and raised her chin.

Rigel could tell she meant it. She slumped her shoulders in defeat and dropped her backpack.

Willow had come prepared. She whipped out a hairbrush she'd concealed somewhere, and before Rigel knew what was what, Willow undid the two braids and started brushing quickly through her hair.

Yank. Yank. *Yank.*

"*Ouch.*"

"It wouldn't have hurt if you'd let me do it before."

Willow's fingers flew down Rigel's back, whipping the new braid together. The hair band snapped into place.

"There. One braid is better." Willow turned Rigel back around and brushed a speck off her shoulder. "You look so much like Lila it's crazy. Quit making that face. You know it's true."

"Found the phone!" Grandma called from somewhere.

"You better get going," Willow said. "Listen, try not to worry. It'll be over before you know it, and I'll see you tonight."

When Willow was nice, it was the best thing ever, but it didn't happen very often anymore.

"Bye!" Rigel shouted, and was out the door and away.

In some ways she was glad school was starting, even if she didn't want to be shut up inside all day long. She'd had the whole month of August off. It had been fun at first. Grandma's chores were easy compared to the work Rigel was used to. But after a while Rigel started to feel like a hamster on an exercise wheel. There were only so many trips you could take to the library and so many afternoons you could spend at the town pool. As for the big town park, it was called the Lee Price Chappell Wilderness, but it was just a few acres full of people walking dogs and moms with strollers.

At least school would give her something to do.

Rigel reminded herself of that while she stood on the

corner of the schoolyard staring up at Orrin P. Fields Middle School.

The school covered a whole block. Three floors of red brick and granite, in the shape of a backward-facing E. FIELDS MIDDLE SCHOOL was carved in a slab of stone over the front double doors. The green lawn in front was sprinkled with people, even this early. Mostly kids, but plenty of parents too. One mom licked her finger and scrubbed something off the cheek of a tall dark-haired boy who batted her hand away and looked around, embarrassed.

Willow was right. Rigel should have worn nicer clothes. Almost all of the kids were in new clothes. They reminded Rigel of freshly peeled hard-boiled eggs, glossy and perfect. The moms had smooth, painted faces and soft hands, and the dads were mostly in business clothes, not work pants and dirty boots.

Maybe it wouldn't have been such a bad idea to have Lila come with her.

Rigel pressed her hand to her shirt. The dog tag was still there.

It'll be over before you know it. That's what Bear had said. Willow too. She repeated it to herself as she marched through the crowd, up the front steps, and into the building.

The dim hallway smelled of floor wax and insecticide and was almost as busy as outside. Voices bounced from wall to wall and off the hard tiled floor.

We need a janitor in the cafeteria—
Who's your math teacher again?—
My mother absolutely freaked—

One end of the hall was emptier and quieter, and her feet took her down that way before her brain could get involved. At the very end was a set of double doors, and she pushed them open and ventured inside to look around.

Maybe Rigel was just a bush rat who hadn't been many places, but even she could recognize this big room as a school cafeteria. There was a stainless steel hatch at one end of the room, with a racket of cheerful voices, rushing water, and clanging pots and pans coming from inside it. There were huge trash and recycling barrels, scuffed linoleum floors, and long tables with benches instead of individual seats. A smell of overcooked vegetables hung over it all.

She backed out, heart pounding again, and leaned against the wall.

She groped for the dog tag again. It was still there.

She definitely should have let Lila come with her.

No! She wasn't a baby. She could do this. She swallowed.

Hocus pocus, time to focus—that was one of Bear's sayings whenever things were getting rough.

Rigel found her binder in her backpack and checked the schedule she'd taped to its inside cover, so she wouldn't forget where to go next.

Fields Middle School Student Schedule
NAME: Harman, Rigel Jane
GRADE: 6th
Student ID#: 571329

Period	Room	Course	Instructor
0	6	Homeroom	Green
1	8	Social Studies	Sapienza
2	13	Spanish	Flores
3	Lab	General Science	Hernandez
4	21	Special Topics	TBA
5	Cafeteria	Lunch	
6	6	Language Arts	Green
7	Gym	Physical Fitness	Maloney
8	23	Mathematics	Trayvick

Homeroom, whatever that was, was in room 6. That sounded like it was on the first floor. Rigel glanced at the number on the nearest classroom door: 14. She made her way slowly back down the hall, staying close to the wall, avoiding looking at anyone so no one would talk to her.

All the way down the hall, past the main office, and across the lobby swarming with kids. There, on the other side, was room 6.

It was still pretty empty, just the way Rigel had wanted it

to be. One boy sat reading a book. He looked up, then went back to reading. A girl was doing something on her phone. Her thumbs flew back and forth across the tiny screen. She didn't even glance over.

New-looking whiteboards gleamed up front. The windows gleamed too. The big bulletin boards were covered with red construction paper decorated with maps, book jackets, and posters. EXPLORING YOUR WORLD THROUGH LANGUAGE ARTS was spelled out along the wall. Rigel chose a desk at the back and settled down. She took out her library book and hid her head in it.

Sneakers shuffled. Hard shoes tapped. The whine of a fluorescent light started up, like a mosquito she couldn't swat. Voices came from all around as the classroom filled with people. Kids talking about summer vacations, teachers and classes, YouTube videos, shopping at the mall . . .

The voices clattered together, but one voice stood out from the jumble.

"Hello," this voice said. "Hello? Hello! *Hello!*"

Three girls stood around Rigel's desk.

They were dressed just alike, in short skirts and striped T-shirts, and they had messenger bags over their shoulders instead of backpacks. And they all had long hair hanging loose, the way Willow wore hers. One girl's wavy dark hair was almost as long as Rigel's. The second was a sugar-white blonde, and the third girl had pale brown hair the color of walnut shells.

"*Finally*," the third girl said. "Hey, do you mind switching seats with me? We want to sit together."

"Oh," Rigel said. "Um, okay—"

"Take your time."

For a moment Rigel thought the girl was being nice, until she rolled her eyes and grinned at her friends.

Rigel pulled her backpack out from under her chair and stood up, and the girl with the pale brown hair slid immediately into the empty seat. She undid her messenger bag and took out a cell phone.

Rigel's book was still on the desk, and she reached out for it.

"Why are you still here, touching my desk?"

"Just getting my book." Rigel was trying to cram *The Evolution of Calpurnia Tate* into her backpack when the door opened and a grown-up, who must have been the teacher, came in.

"Everyone find a seat, please," she said.

Rigel went to the closest desk, in the row next to the window.

The teacher had a round, pale, soft-looking face like an under-baked cookie, and brown hair that was mixed with silvery strands and pulled into a bun at the back of her head. She wore a knee-length blue dress and the kind of silvery jewelry that Willow called "arty."

She picked up a marker and wrote on the whiteboard. *Cynthia Green.* The smell of the marker drifted over to Rigel.

"I'm Mrs. Green, and I'm going to be your homeroom

teacher this year. We're going to be running a few minutes long today. We have a lot to get through, but let's start with our roll call."

Rigel snuck another look at her schedule.

Not only was Mrs. Green down for homeroom, she was Rigel's Language Arts teacher too.

Meanwhile, Mrs. Green sat behind her desk, flipped open a notebook with pale green pages, and picked up a pencil.

"Anand, Lily."

"Here," the girl sitting across from Rigel called.

"Brooker, Sylvie."

"B-B-B-Brookner," a girl said. Her desk was two seats in front of Rigel. Her golden-brown hair was barely contained in a bushy ponytail, and her thick glasses were parked halfway down her nose.

"I'm sorry." Mrs. Green scribbled in her roll book. "Carling, Marion."

"Here." It was the girl with long dark hair.

"DiNapoli, Samuel."

"Here," said the boy sitting behind Sylvie Brookner. He had a gentle expression and a big belly that rounded out the front of his first-day-of-school polo shirt. "Call me Sam."

It was hot. Rigel plucked at her jeans and wondered whether the skirt would have been such a bad idea after all.

"Elia, Jacob."

"Yeah. Call me Jake."

"Foyle, Hayden."

"Here," the girl with light brown hair said, leaning back comfortably in what should have been Rigel's seat.

"Green, Corey."

"Here," the boy in front of Rigel said, turning sideways in his seat. Rigel recognized him as the embarrassed boy out front whose mom had tried to spit-shine his cheek.

Mrs. Green joked with Corey about how they both had the same last name and were probably related somehow. Corey Green acted as if this were a terrifying prospect.

Here it came: Mrs. Green was about to call Rigel's name—

"Han, Julie."

"Here." This girl had shoulder-length hair and round glasses that gave her face a look of good-natured surprise.

Rigel was so happy about her momentary reprieve that she smiled at Julie Han, like they were old friends. Julie offered a smile of her own back.

"Harman, Rigel."

She couldn't believe it. Mrs. Green had mispronounced her name. *Rye-Gull*, Mrs. Green had said. Like Rigel was a seabird.

She cleared her throat. "It's Rigel," she near-whispered.

"Speak up, please."

"It's not Rye-Gull. It's Rye-Jil."

"All right. Rigel." Mrs. Green ticked something in her notebook. Then—just as Rigel relaxed—she went on. "Now, I understand from the office that your family just moved to Baldwin this summer. Is that right?"

Rigel touched her dog tag, as if touching it would summon Bear to stand beside her. "Yeah. I guess so."

"You guess so?" Mrs. Green said, and a low ripple of laughter ran around the room.

Rigel hadn't said that because she was stupid. She'd said it because she wasn't sure what you would call them now, living without Bear. Whether they were still a family without him.

"You *know* so—am I right? We're going to be friendly, everybody, and help Rigel feel at home. Where did you move from, Rigel?"

"Alaska."

A mutter of excitement bubbled up at the word "Alaska." Sam glanced over his shoulder, raising his eyebrows in a friendly way.

"Very interesting. Where are you from in Alaska?" Mrs. Green asked. "Anchorage? Fairbanks?"

Should she say Galena? Or Fort McPhee? She bet no one here would know where those places were. And she was too nervous to talk anyway.

Mrs. Green gestured to the map at the front of the room. "Why don't you show us?"

Rigel kept her head down, so she only saw her classmates' shoes as she passed. She pointed to an empty spot north of the Yukon, between Galena and Fort McPhee. Her hand shook from the thought of so many eyes on her back. She hoped no one noticed.

"I see," Mrs. Green said. "Close to Fairbanks."

They weren't close to Fairbanks, but Rigel didn't correct her. She zoomed back to her seat.

A grinning boy put up his hand.

"What's your name?" Mrs. Green asked.

"Davis Rogers," the boy said, sounding a little surprised, like she should have already known who he was. "You know what? My uncle went hunting in Alaska last year. He got a bighorn sheep!"

He got a *Dall* sheep, Rigel corrected him, but only to herself.

Hunting was a major topic of conversation in Fort McPhee, something she knew how to talk about. This could be a lucky break, her chance to make a friend. "My dad started letting me hunt on my own this year," she said to Davis.

"With a *gun?*" Davis said.

"Well, yeah, we don't bowhunt. Do you?" She was ready to be impressed if he did. Bowhunting was hard-core, Bear always said that.

"Oh, right," the boy behind Davis said. Jake, that was his name. He sat back in his seat and crossed his arms. "What kind of gun did you use, then." He spoke flatly, like he was catching her out in a lie.

"A .22," Rigel said. A silence followed this. "Just for rabbits and spruce chickens, stuff like that. Bear said I was old enough."

"Who's Bear?"

"My dad."

"You call your dad by his *first name?*"

"This is all very interesting," Mrs. Green cut in, "but we'd better get on with roll call."

The glare of the spotlight was finally off Rigel, but not before someone whispered, from across the room, "Show-off."

She turned to see who had said it. Hayden Foyle looked back and leaned sideways to whisper something to her two friends. Then they all stared over unblinkingly.

Wonderful.

Why didn't she just stay quiet? Why had she tried to say anything?

Worrying the whole thing over, she missed most of the rest of the class names, although she did notice that Hayden Foyle's second friend, the blond girl, was named Celeste Schenk. Rigel thought "Schenk" was kind of a funny-sounding name, but no one laughed. Celeste glanced around coolly, like she was daring anyone to try.

Next Mrs. Green passed out thick booklets with colored covers. The School Handbook. Then there came another bunch of handouts that Mrs. Green started explaining one by one.

Rigel looked through the window, studying the oak tree outside. Its thin leaves swished back and forth in a light breeze she couldn't feel.

They'd never had a first day of school back in Alaska. When the correspondence schoolwork arrived, you got to work, whatever day that was. You spread your books out on the table after breakfast and studied. If you needed to get up and stretch, you did. If you wanted to go outside for a breath of fresh air, you went. When you were done with your lessons, you were done for the day.

331 days left in Connecticut.

331 days was going to be a long time if every day was like this. Rigel shifted her butt on the hard chair.

A bird flew down from one of the lower branches of the oak.

A crow. Nothing special. Crows were to ravens what Connecticut was to Alaska: more dumb, more ordinary, and a lot smaller.

The bird cocked its head to study something, then headed toward Rigel's window.

It had a spray of white feathers just above its bill, between its bright, dark gray eyes. Could crows have white feathers?

Maybe it was some other kind of bird.

But it acted like a crow, hopping around briskly. It came back into sight holding something brown in its bill—

Ah. The crow had found a chunk of doughnut. It pinned the treat down with one claw and pecked away.

Why was it staying on the ground? It was much safer to eat up in the tree.

Something startled the bird, and it took off. But it didn't fly the way it should have flown, with a powerful, easy downbeat of its wings. It scrambled up into the tree, favoring one wing.

Rigel stood up and leaned closer to the window to get a better look.

"Rigel!" Mrs. Green said.

Rigel jumped and banged her knee against the side of her desk. It hurt. She collapsed into her seat, grabbed her knee, and rocked back and forth.

"What's so interesting out that window?"

"A crow," she said through gritted teeth.

"A crow." Something about the way Mrs. Green repeated the words made people snicker. "And what was I talking about, while you were watching this crow?"

Rigel froze. A low whisper came from Corey Green in the seat in front of her: *Library tour.*

"The library tour," Rigel repeated.

Mrs. Green relaxed a little bit. "All right. But, Rigel, in this class, we stay seated, we don't stand up and move around without getting permission first."

Rigel's face got hot.

"All right, class, make sure you finish reading the handbook tonight. Welcome to middle school."

The bell rang.

Rigel put her hands over her ears—that piercing noise drove straight into her head—but none of the other kids even seemed to notice. They just jumped up and stuffed their handouts into their backpacks. It was time to go on to the next class.

Chapter 7

Every few minutes all morning, through Social Studies and Spanish, General Science and Special Topics, Rigel flicked open her binder and studied her schedule, just to make sure Lunch was still there. It always was.

She'd been dreading lunchtime ever since she saw the cafeteria. Especially those long tables, which meant that even on the first day of school, you had to sit with other people—people you didn't know yet.

Strangers.

And then there was Willow's lecture about the right place to sit. But how would you pick this table, and what would you do if they didn't want you sitting there? Rigel suspected Davis, the boy whose uncle hunted Dall sheep, was one of the right people. He looked too relaxed to be anything else. But how could she tell for sure?

By the time Special Topics was over, Rigel didn't think she'd be able to eat anything anyway. But when she came out into the hall, she noticed something interesting.

Not everyone was going to the cafeteria.

Most people were. A rowdy, steady stream of kids was headed in that direction, like a flock of noisy birds. But some went the opposite way. Not as many, but a definite ant trail headed somewhere else, somewhere that wasn't the cafeteria.

Rigel followed those kids. They led her down the empty main hall, left at the gym, and down another hall to the big double doors marked SCHOOL LIBRARY.

The study tables inside the library were already full of sixth graders, one to a table, with their lunch boxes open. Rigel was about to sit in a beanbag chair when she noticed a familiar girl at one of the tables. It was the girl who came before Rigel in the homeroom roll call—Julie Han.

Rigel summoned her courage and went across to Julie's table. Julie glanced up from her book, then stacked up her scatter of handouts and folders to clear a space.

Rigel sat down and unzipped her lunch box. Now she was glad she had packed a boring turkey sandwich.

"I'm Julie," the girl reminded her in a whisper.

"Rigel."

"Girls," the librarian said. "Usually I don't mind quiet talking, but we're having a meeting right now."

The nameplate on her desk said MRS. LEIBMANN. She went back to the talk she was giving a bunch of serious-looking big kids standing around her.

Julie wrinkled her nose. "Probably library aides," she whispered. "My brother, Danny, did that in eighth grade—"

"Girls."

Julie flashed a smile at Rigel, shrugged, and went back to her book.

Rigel's stomach growled. She bit into her sandwich. Even in Connecticut, you had to eat.

卌

That night at dinner, Grandma and Lila had questions about school.

"Did you like your teacher, Izzy?"

"He's a *man!*" Izzy said. "Mr. Murphy! He put on music after circle time and we all got to dance!"

"Did your classmates seem nice?"

"We did the monkey bars! Jazmin and me! We went all the way across and then back again!"

"Did you like the hot lunch?" Grandma asked.

Izzy had thought hot lunch was the most exciting idea ever, so Lila said she could try it for a few days.

"We had beefaroni!" Izzy said. "And fruit cup with pineapple!"

Izzy loved pineapple.

"Was there anything you *didn't* like?" Grandma asked.

Izzy took her time thinking it over. "School smells funny."

The grown-ups laughed, but Rigel and Willow didn't. School *did* smell funny. It smelled like cleaning products and hot-lunch fumes and dry-erase markers and whatever perfume the teacher was wearing.

"How about you, Willow?" Lila asked. "How did it go for you?"

"It was pretty okay," Willow said. "Art looks like it's going to be sort of epic. Our teacher, Mrs. Kravets, has an MFA and she's even had her paintings in shows. I already signed up for Art Club and the first meeting is this week. And—there was one boy . . ."

Willow trailed off and studied her plate.

"Yes?" Grandma said at last.

"Well, it was so crowded in the halls that I got lost right before third period. I knew I was going to be late, and I was seriously stressing, and then this one boy noticed and he stopped and helped me figure out where to go next. He was nice." Willow stole a glance at all of them. "And cute. He told me I should sit with him and his friends at lunch, so I did. All of Christian's friends play sports, they're all going out for teams this year. Christian plays football. And runs track."

"Is that his name?" Lila asked, smiling.

"Christian Tallmadge." Willow said it as if they were the two most beautiful words in English. "*Not* Chris. *Christian.*"

Grandma said, "How about you, Rye? How was school?"

Everyone waited for her to answer.

Rigel forked baked ziti into her mouth and chewed it carefully.

Forks clicked on plates. The black-cat clock over the stove ticked. Cars swooshed by outside.

Grandma finally said, "Rigel, tell us one thing about your first day of school. Then we'll leave you alone."

"I saw a crow."

Willow laughed her tinkly new laugh. She probably practiced it to make herself sound like a popular girl. "I thought we were talking about *school*."

"I saw the crow *at* school. Unless it was some other kind of bird. It was shaped like a crow, and it acted like a crow, but it had white markings right here." Rigel tapped the bridge of her nose.

"You see crows with white feathers now and then," Grandma remarked. "When I was growing up, there was a pure-white crow in our neighborhood one spring. We were all amazed. But it didn't stick around for very long."

That wasn't surprising. A snow-white crow would stick out like a sore thumb, easy pickings for a hawk or an owl. It was better to blend in.

School was probably the same way.

"There's a place two blocks from here along the railroad tracks that's a crow roost. I'm glad it's not closer." Grandma shook her head. "Those birds are destructive! One year they dug up an entire row of my Brandywine tomatoes, just for fun. I went out and chased them away and they came right back."

"White markings can be hereditary," Lila said, helping Izzy pour her second glass of milk. "Or they can come from an injury or a nutritional deficiency."

Rigel remembered the crow tearing into its doughnut. No wonder it was suffering from a nutritional deficiency. In the meantime, it had gotten her off the hook and she felt a flash of gratitude toward it. Maybe the crow would be back around school tomorrow.

Chapter 8

Countdown day 314.

There was a postcard for Rigel on the kitchen table. A dull picture of Pump Station #1 at Prudhoe Bay, showing green tundra rolling out behind the low gray buildings.

"He could have at least sent a polar bear postcard," Willow said, pouring boiling water into her tea mug.

But the picture didn't matter. What mattered were the words scribbled on the back: *Time is passing real quick up here. Hope you are staying busy and cheerful. See you SOON.* Rigel knew what that SOON meant. It meant that their deal was still on. She put it away carefully in her backpack.

"You're just jealous," she remarked. Willow hadn't gotten anything from Bear.

"Oh, I'm dying of jealousy." Willow held up an envelope and smirked.

Willow had gotten a letter that day, not a postcard, and to rub it in, the letter was from Adela John, Kimora's older sister. Adela and Willow had barely been friends. But here Willow was, getting fat letters from Adela while Kimora hardly sent Rigel anything, just a few short emails.

Rigel had email now through school. They made you set it up, whether you wanted it or not.

"Any news from Fort McPhee?" Rigel asked.

"Like what? Nothing ever happens there."

No one hearing Willow talk now would guess that she had once jumped on chances to visit Fort McPhee, or Galena, or anywhere else you could call a town. Rigel was sure the letter was full of bush news. It wasn't like Adela would have any other kind. But Rigel wasn't going to beg.

She went out to the dining room and picked up her boots from the mat by the side door.

"Where are you going?" Willow called, but Rigel just let the door bang shut behind her as she left the house.

Let Willow figure it out.

She sat on the stoop to put on her boots and lace them up, sniffing the air, which was clean and dry.

Rigel had a chore for this afternoon—a real chore, not boring inside work like folding laundry or mopping floors.

The winter firewood had been delivered earlier in the week. The men from the hardware store had just dumped it on Grandma's driveway, the logs too big to burn and not even stacked to stay dry. That was just plain slack. It wouldn't have flown if Bear had been around. But Rigel had volunteered right away to get the wood split and stacked.

She liked splitting wood.

And today was Friday, so she didn't have to do homework. She had plenty of time to get it done.

Rigel went into the garage and got the tools she needed: the short-handled sledgehammer, an ax, and the splitting wedges. Aside from a little dust, everything was clean and in good order. These were her grandfather's tools. Rigel had never met him, but clearly he knew about splitting wood.

The chopping block was an old hardwood stump that usually stayed beside the garage. She rolled it out onto the driveway.

She put the first log onto the chopping block and waggled it to make sure it was stable. She found the best hairline crack in the log and fit a splitting wedge into the crack. Then Rigel raised the sledgehammer and brought it down.

Lila could split wood with a ten-pound maul. That split a log in one or two goes. But Rigel wasn't strong enough to handle the maul for more than a swing or two. It took her longer to split logs with the five-pound sledgehammer, but it worked just fine.

A few blows of the sledgehammer onto the splitting wedge, and the log split into two halves with that familiar *clunk* of sundering wood. The split halves rattled down onto Grandma's driveway.

That sound took Rigel back to Alaska, where they heated the cabin with spruce. In the winter, their stove went through wood at an amazing clip. They dragged in logs with the snow machine, and Bear cut those logs into smaller segments with a chain saw. But the chain saw used gasoline, and gasoline was expensive. So the rest of the chopping got done by hand.

Rigel didn't mind doing it. She'd take doing splits over packing water any day.

Besides, she was getting paid. The girls were paid for their weekly chores now. That was how they got pocket money. You could do the chores yourself, or get one of your sisters to do them and let them earn the money. Lila and Grandma didn't care, as long as the work got done. That was how it worked. Lately Rigel was making major coin picking up Willow's housework, because all Willow wanted to do in her spare time was talk on the phone to Christian Tallmadge or hang out at his house.

Rigel wanted to go back to Alaska with some money in her pocket. Maybe even pay for her own ticket home. Bear would be impressed if she could do that.

She picked up the next log, put it on the chopping block, and steadied it. Placed the wedge, raised the sledgehammer, and let it drop.

You got into a rhythm with splitting wood. The split wood piled up around her feet. She could smell it.

Clunk rattle rattle. Clunk rattle rattle. Clunk rattle rattle.

The weight of the sledgehammer made her arms burn.

But just when it was getting painful, it was time to take a break from the chopping and stack the just-split wood along the side of the garage, handy to the house. She went back and forth, humming.

Caw-caw.

A crow perched on one of the fence posts of Grandma's vegetable garden, its head turned, watching her.

Rigel cawed back: *Ah-ah.*

The crow stretched. The wing and leg on one side, then the wing and leg on the other, and then one final stretch, spreading out both wings. It stood still, then scrabbled with its bill into the feathers over one leg.

"Lice bothering you?" Rigel asked.

The crow cawed loudly.

"Hey, I'm not judging."

With a last dignified look, the bird pushed up and off into flight. There was not a speck of white anywhere on its glossy blackness.

That white-splotched crow at school had been the only one she'd ever seen with different coloration. And she had only seen it that one time, even though she'd kept an eye peeled for it.

Probably something had gotten it.

Clunk rattle rattle.

Poor little guy.

Rigel put another log on the block.

Clunk rattle rattle.

She kicked the newly split wood away from the chopping block and set up her next log. She lifted the sledgehammer—

"Hey, *Harman!*"

Rigel jumped, and her stroke with the sledgehammer went wrong. The hammer clipped the edge of the log, instead of the center, and the log rocketed into the depths of Grandma's garage. Something went *smash* back there. Rigel dropped the sledgehammer and jumped away from the chopping block. She slipped on a piece of split wood and almost fell.

A burst of laughter came from behind her.

Davis and Jake, those two boys from homeroom, were sitting on their bikes at the end of her driveway. They had their helmets loosened and pushed back.

"What are you *doing?*" Davis asked her, flashing his big, quick grin, the one everyone in sixth grade admired. Davis was definitely one of the right people. She couldn't imagine sitting at his table during lunch.

"What are *you* doing?" Rigel shot back. She picked up the sledgehammer from the ground. "Don't you know better than to sneak up on someone using a sledgehammer?"

The boys looked at each other. Rigel realized that they really hadn't known. But her heart was still pounding at the thought of what that sledgehammer might have done to her leg.

"We just wondered what you were up to." Jake was short and chunky, with curly brown hair. The kind of boy the girls at school called "cute."

"Do some more," Davis ordered. And then he got an idea.

Rigel could practically see it pop up into his big dumb brain. He took off his helmet and let the fancy bike drop onto the driveway like a few scratches on it didn't even matter. "Hey, let me try."

"No. Way," Rigel said.

"Give me that," Davis said, coming up the driveway.

For a moment, she was tempted to hand the sledgehammer over and let Davis look like a fool.

But what if he hurt himself?

"No. You don't know what you're doing."

The next thing she knew his arms were around her and he was trying to wrestle the hammer away. She couldn't believe anyone could possibly be that stupid, but Davis Rogers was. His breath was warm on her face and smelled like mint.

The screen door squeaked open.

Davis froze.

"What's going on?" Willow stood on the stoop.

Rigel pulled the sledgehammer away from Davis and set it down by the chopping block.

"Um . . . just messing around. Who are you?" Davis added that question in a rush.

Willow tilted her head to one side, the way Hayden Foyle liked to do, and said nothing.

"That's my sister," Rigel said.

Why couldn't Willow have brown hair, and be pale and skinny? And Rigel could be tall and blond and curvy, just to see what that was like. Even for one day.

"Well, see you." Davis practically ran back down the driveway to his bike. He yanked it upright and climbed on.

"Dude!" Willow called. "Your *helmet*."

Davis got back off the bike and scooped up his helmet. He was blushing. Davis Rogers, the prince of sixth grade, was blushing. He shot away down their street, Jake pedaling hard to keep up.

Willow pushed her hair away from her face and gave a secret little smile. "Lila called. She's bringing home pizza. Why don't you clean up your tools and come on inside?"

"You don't have to tell *me* to clean up my tools," Rigel snapped.

She stomped into the garage, where she found two smashed clay flowerpots that needed to be cleared away.

IIII

It turned out that the pizza was for a celebration, because Lila had found work.

"That's wonderful, Lila!" Grandma said. "Tell us all about it. Which job did you get?"

"Well," Lila began, "it's kind of a funny story. I was helping Dr. Morgan take his garbage cans to the curb this morning—"

Dr. Morgan lived alone, two doors down from them. He used a cane to get around, and he and his house shared the same shabby, neglected look.

"—and he was telling me that he needed a cleaner, and I was telling him that I needed a job. And then it occurred to both of us that maybe we could help each other out. I start Monday."

Start what? Rigel wondered. Did Dr. Morgan know of a lab job that Lila could have? The silence stretched out until Izzy broke it.

"I don't get it."

"I'm cleaning Dr. Morgan's house, honey," Lila said.

Cleaning someone's house? Lila had a college degree. She was supposed to get a job in a lab or a science department. Someplace where she wore a white coat and held up test tubes, the way scientists did on TV.

"Oh!" Grandma hesitated. "Well, that's—that's good news."

Lila studied Grandma over the rim of her water glass. "Better than nothing?"

"You surprised me. But, honestly, it's a practical decision. We could use the money, and I've heard it's always better to be working while you job hunt."

"And it's not forever," Lila said. "I hope."

Willow put down her pizza slice. "So, when people ask me what my mom does, I get to tell them she cleans houses. Wonderful."

Lila wasn't Rigel's favorite person at the moment, but, still, Rigel didn't think that was fair. Work was work. Anything that paid a steady income was a good job. Rigel knew about some jobs, like working the slime line in a cannery, that were a lot nastier than cleaning toilets and dusting furniture.

Although Rigel was pretty surprised people could feel rich enough to pay someone else to clean their houses.

"I don't see what's wrong with it," she said.

"Of course *you* wouldn't," Willow snapped. "Why does everyone in this family have to embarrass me? You know what *my* news is today? Christian asked me to be his girlfriend, right after lunch when he was walking me to class. I should be feeling happy right now! I was happy, all day! And now this."

Boyfriend? Already? Actually, though, it wasn't that surprising. Look at how Davis Rogers had fallen all over himself just because Willow talked to him.

Grandma and Lila glanced at each other. They'd be discussing this development later, Rigel guessed, sitting outside at the picnic table with glasses of wine, the way they did sometimes.

"Willow would prefer for me to sit around the house and feel depressed." Lila speared a slice of cucumber out of the salad. "Instead, I'm going to get busy and make us some money."

Flushing pink, Willow stared down at her plate.

Rigel would have felt sorry for her, if she hadn't been so obnoxious lately.

Chapter 9

"Cheerleader tryouts will be this Wednesday after school," blared out from the loudspeaker in the corner of the classroom.

Eighth graders did the announcements. Apparently, it was some kind of privilege. If anyone ever made Rigel read news snippets about bake sales and team tryouts, it would be more like a punishment.

"A new school club is starting! The Fencing Club will have its first meeting . . ."

Rigel sank into her seat, staring out the window.

Countdown day 311.

311 days left in Connecticut.

It was still only September, and school didn't let out until late June. It was going to be a long nine months. Rigel reminded herself that she had already lasted 54 days, not 20 percent of the total 365, but also way more than 10 percent. She started her usual calculations to come up with the exact percentage, but the numbers faded as fast she came up with them. It was like the hot, stale air stole them away.

She yawned and looked out the window again. Then she sat straight up.

The white-marked crow skittered over the grass with something in its beak. Not a chunk of doughnut this time, but something wiggling. Maybe a worm. Maybe an insect. Rigel knew better than to stand up, so she couldn't take a closer look. But the crow was there. That was the main thing. It was still alive.

Well, how about that?

Rigel didn't know she'd spoken out loud until Corey, sitting in front of her, whispered, "How about *what?*"

"Are you talking to me?" Rigel whispered back.

Corey turned around. "You're the one who said, 'Well, how about that?' What were *you* talking about?"

Mrs. Green said, "Corey, we're listening to morning announcements. A little quiet, please?"

"Sorry," Corey said.

The speaker crackled out, "There's been a change of school policy about food in the school library. No more food is allowed in the library due to concerns about pest problems."

"*What?*" Corey said at the very moment Rigel muttered, "Oh, wonderful."

"Students can still use the library at lunch, but all food and drinks are banned," the announcer intoned.

Rigel and Corey groaned at the same time.

Ⅲ̶

At lunchtime Rigel lingered at her desk in Special Topics, and when she finally went into the main hall, it was deserted.

She made a quick trip to her locker for her lunch, then went around the corner, past the teachers' bathroom and the nurse's office. There was a stairwell there that always seemed empty except for class changes. She sat down on the steps and unzipped her lunch box.

Her sandwich was leftover roast beef from Sunday dinner. It was okay with horseradish on it.

Even Rigel had to admit Connecticut supermarkets were great. You could get fresh vegetables and fruit whenever you wanted, anything from bananas to avocados, not to mention fresh milk, juice, eggs, and yogurt. The cereal and snack aisles went on forever, and the prices were low compared to Alaskan markets.

But the meat was terrible!

Supermarket meat didn't taste like anything compared to wild meat. Chicken was the worst, because it didn't have enough fat. Fat was what made meat taste good. If anyone had ever served a boneless, skinless chicken breast to their old friend Wilfred he would have thought that person was crazy, or else plenty stingy.

"Rigel!" Mrs. Green stood in the hall with an armful of folders. "Why are you eating on the steps? I would have thought this morning's announcement was clear enough for anyone."

"It said we couldn't eat in the library," Rigel said.

Mrs. Green raised her eyebrows and waited.

"It didn't say anything about the hallway."

"The cafeteria is the place where we eat in this building." Mrs. Green spoke slowly, as if Rigel might not understand if she spoke any faster. "Now, take your lunch and go there. Food in the hall attracts pests."

The food sat in their lockers all morning long attracting pests, Rigel almost said, but stopped herself in time.

Maybe Mrs. Green would turn away now and go to the faculty lounge, where all the other teachers were. Rigel could just go ahead and finish eating, while she worried about where to eat lunch tomorrow.

But Mrs. Green didn't move. She stood there, making sure Rigel went where she was supposed to.

It was a stupid rule, with no good reason behind it. That's what Bear always said school was like—all kinds of dumb rules and no one caring what the kids thought about any of it. Rigel threw her sandwich into her lunch box. Then she marched down the hallway to her locker, crammed her lunch box back inside, and stomped past Mrs. Green in the direction of the library.

"Rigel!"

She set her face into a polite expression before she turned around.

Mrs. Green's eyebrows knit, her nostrils flared. "You are being very rude, young lady, and I don't appreciate it. At all."

Rigel pursed her lips. "Can I go to the library now?"

"*May* I," Mrs. Green threw back.

"*May* I go to the library?" Rigel spoke very clearly, as if she were nailing each word to the wall.

"Yes, you *may* go to the library."

Rigel could feel Mrs. Green's gaze on her back all the way past the office, the sixth-grade lockers, several classrooms, and the gym. Once she turned the corner, at least she was out of Mrs. Green's sight. She was glad to see the library doors at the end of the hallway, but . . .

She didn't want to go inside.

Really, Rigel might go out of her mind if she had to sit in another hot room under fluorescent lights that buzzed like the world's biggest mosquitoes.

The library doors opened and Mr. Lincoln, the custodian, came out with a broom and bucket. Mr. Lincoln was short and round, with a shaved head and a quiet smile. Even though he spent all day cleaning up other people's messes, he always whistled softly as he worked, and he already knew every sixth grader at Fields Middle by name. He ducked into the custodian's closet and came out without the mop bucket. He smiled as he passed her, heading for the faculty lounge. "Time for my lunch, Rigel!"

She had passed that closet dozens of times, but today she stopped short to study the door. Just a plain scuffed wooden door with a sign that said CUSTODIAN'S CLOSET.

But maybe there was somewhere to sit in there. And at least it would be a change from the library.

Rigel hesitated. She rehearsed an excuse in case she disturbed anyone, and then tried the doorknob.

The closet door was unlocked. The custodians probably thought that no one would be interested in their mop buckets and push brooms and gallon bottles of cleaning products. Those things didn't interest Rigel either, but there was one thing in the custodian's closet that interested her a lot.

It was a door, a metal door with a push bar, the kind of door that led outside.

And unlike all the other side doors at school, this door had no sign saying EMERGENCY EXIT ONLY. ALARM WILL SOUND.

Rigel pushed the door open, and a gust of cool damp air blew into her face. Nothing rang or buzzed. She stepped outside, onto an old concrete patio with edges that were crumbling away.

This faced the back of their school, an area mainly taken up by the teachers' parking lot. Across the patchy grass, a tangle of witch hazel and holly trees grew next to the sidewalk, and there were plenty of tall skinny maples shooting up toward the sun. On the right was a busy road, where cars whooshed by on the other side of a long row of pine trees planted along the sidewalk. To her left was the parking lot, the cafeteria dumpster, and an overgrown garden plot full of chin-high weeds and old cornstalks.

After school drop-off, there was no one out here until the teachers left at the end of the workday.

If Rigel was watchful and quiet, no one would know she was out here either.

She could barely believe her luck.

She carefully put a book between the door and its jamb, so the door couldn't click shut. Then she spread out her arms, closed her eyes, and just enjoyed the feel of the wind on her face for a while. Finally, she sat on the crumbling step.

She wished she had her lunch. She'd make sure she had it in her backpack tomorrow, because she had found her new lunch spot. No more worries about the cafeteria for her.

A scrabbling noise came from the dumpster.

A crow emerged from inside.

The doughnut-lover with the white markings. It hopped awkwardly down onto the parking lot asphalt with a greasy wad of paper.

"So this is your new hangout?" Rigel asked.

The crow gave her a wary look, then tore the paper open with several determined pecks. There was half of a chicken filet sandwich inside. The crow pulled loose a long gob of lettuce smeared with mayonnaise.

"Ugh. That's disgusting."

It wasn't easy horking the lettuce down, but the crow managed.

Next, it pinned down the filet with one foot and tore a hunk of chicken loose.

Ravens liked garbage when they could get it. They liked dog food too. They'd team up in pairs to get it, one raven to distract the dog while the other snatched up a mouthful. And they were real nuisances around fish camps in the summer, filching the drying fish off the racks. So this crow ate chicken sandwiches out of the dumpster instead of drying salmon. Well, it was a Connecticut crow, not an Alaskan raven. It had to eat what it could find, second-rate food in this second-rate place.

Still, it was wrong for a wild animal to hang around and eat nothing but human leavings.

A Fort McPhee word came into Rigel's mind: *hutlaanee.*

Hutlaanee was a Koyukon Athabascan word, one everyone in Fort McPhee knew, even someone like Rigel who didn't even live there anymore and wasn't Native. It meant taboo, sort of. Bad luck. Something that was wrong or dangerous. It meant all of those things and none of them, because none of them was exactly right.

That dumpster-diving crow wasn't the only thing around here that felt wrong.

Rigel stared over at the glittering ranks of cars in the parking lot.

At the houses across the street, lined up one after another, perched facing forward, each on its own little patch of grass.

Orange skies at night, pavement everywhere anyone looked, honking horns and ringing bells . . .

She pressed her dog tag against her chest.

How could you live somewhere where everything was wrong and made you feel sick?

Well, you could. Because Rigel was doing it.

The crow flapped painfully back up into the dumpster. It didn't look as if its wing was much better.

||||

Rigel knew what it was like to be hungry. Not because Lila and Bear didn't provide, but because unexpected things happened in the Bush. A snowshoe binding might snap, or a boat motor might quit, or Bear might just forget to bring food. He was absentminded that way and Lila sometimes reminded him that even if he could go all day without eating, the girls couldn't. Rigel could remember times when she had been a lot hungrier than she was that afternoon.

But that didn't really help when you were sitting in math class with your stomach rumbling so loudly you were afraid the other kids could hear it.

Rigel searched through her backpack and found an old

box of raisins. They were so dried out they were more like raisin-flavored pebbles, but she munched on them anyway.

Mr. Trayvick was going over yesterday's decimal problems at the board. He had shoulder-length red hair and round wire-rim glasses and was young enough to still have pimples sometimes. "Zitface," Davis and Jake called him.

"Now, many of you forgot to shift your decimal points and ended up making errors because of that. Common newbie mistake. There's an easy way to make this problem go away, and someone in this class already knows the trick. She used it yesterday on her homework, if I deciphered her handwriting correctly. Rigel, would you like to come up here and show off your hack? Try this problem." He scrawled $17 \div 0.2$ on the whiteboard.

Rigel swallowed the last of the raisins. Forgetting the rule about never eating in class, she dropped the empty box on her desk. Mr. Trayvick raised his eyebrows and didn't say anything, but some of the other kids laughed.

She held her breath against the fumes of the dry-erase marker. She wrote quickly under $17 \div 0.2$:

$170 \div 2$

85

She circled 85, capped the marker, and let out her breath.

"Correct. Can you explain what you did there?"

She talked to Mr. Trayvick, instead of all the other people in the room. That way, she didn't get nervous. "You just multiply both numbers by ten until the decimal point goes away. It doesn't affect the result because you're doing it to both the dividend and the divisor." Math was another area where Lila liked them using proper words.

Mr. Trayvick nodded. "Exactly."

"Dividend, divisor, and dork," Hayden said from her seat at the back of the room.

"Hayden, thank you for volunteering," Mr. Trayvick said brightly. "Get on up here and give this one a try." He wrote $19 \div 0.5$ on the board.

Hayden walked slowly to the whiteboard and gave Rigel a really dirty look before picking up the marker.

HHT

Once school was finally over, Rigel sat down on the stone bench under the oak in front and took out her lunch to eat right then and there.

"Hey, Rigel." It was Julie Han from homeroom. "I thought you took the bus."

Rigel's mouth was too full to talk. She struggled to chew and swallow. "No, I walk home. That way."

"I do too. It's weird I never see you on the way home."

That was Rigel's fault. If she didn't run out of school at the end of every day and jog half the way home, she and Julie would have seen each other at dismissal before now.

Julie hiked her backpack up. "Did you hear the

announcement about fencing this morning? About starting a school club? I'm totally asking my parents about doing it."

Rigel imagined Julie in a face mask, slashing out with a sword. "That does sound cool."

"I went and talked to Mr. Brodeur about it. He says you don't have to try out or anything, just show up. He says he wants to start a team, but a club's the first step."

Maybe Rigel should give fencing a try. It wasn't like she had much else to do, once her homework and chores were done. It would help fill up the long boring days until she was back in Alaska.

"Hey, want to walk home together?" Rigel asked. Willow would be proud.

Julie smiled. "Okay, but can you eat while you walk? My mom goes apes if I'm even five minutes late."

Rigel had just finished her sandwich anyway. She got out her cheese crackers to share with Julie as they walked.

It turned out that Julie's parents owned the stationery store downtown, and Julie went there every day, unless she had something going on at school. She did chores in the shop.

Julie helped herself to a cracker from Rigel's baggie. "Why are you eating lunch after school anyway? Did you have a club meeting or something?"

The idea of being in a club made Rigel laugh.

"What's so funny?" Julie bit into another cracker. "I have Stage Club every other Wednesday during lunch. If Mrs.

Pitera didn't break the rules and let us eat in the auditorium, I'd starve."

"Nothing like that. It's just Mrs. Green caught me eating in the hall and tried to send me to the cafeteria. I wouldn't go, so I—" Rigel stopped herself just in time from mentioning her new secret outdoor spot. If a teacher ever found out about it, there would be an alarm on that door in no time. "I missed lunch," she finished, feeling idiotic.

Julie nodded. "And you know something? If you were Hayden Foyle, or one of her friends, Mrs. Green wouldn't have done anything. She totally sucks up to them."

Rigel had never noticed. But the moment Julie pointed it out, she knew it was true. There was this way Mrs. Green had of smiling at Hayden, and complimenting her clothes, and asking her to run errands to the office or to another classroom. "Definitely," she agreed.

"It's like Mrs. Green thinks Hayden's going to invite her over for a sleepover or something." Julie mashed the call button on the traffic light with more force than seemed necessary.

"What's Hayden's deal, anyway?"

"Oh, she likes running the show. My brother, Danny, says some popular kids are like that. We used to call her Princess in elementary school. One mistake, and it's off with your head. Listen," Julie went on quickly, like she wanted to change the subject, "you can always eat with us in the cafeteria, you know. Us stage nerds, the kids in orchestra and chorale and theater. We're so low on the pecking order anyone can eat with us."

That might be a good option for rainy days. "Is that why you stopped eating lunch in the library?"

Julie hadn't eaten there in weeks.

"That was just for the first few days, till I knew where to sit in the cafeteria. Didn't want to make a mistake on the first day. Danny gave me that advice."

"My sister Willow told me to eat in the cafeteria, but to make sure I sat at the right table."

"How are you supposed to know the right table on the first day?"

"Exactly!" Rigel exclaimed. "That's what I said!"

"What can I tell you? I'm a genius." Julie took the last cracker out of Rigel's baggie and popped it into her mouth. They were standing on a corner, and Julie pointed toward downtown. "I go that way."

"Oh." Rigel nodded toward the houses north of their corner. "I go that way."

"Hey, do you want to come to my house and have a tea or something?"

"Really?" Rigel said. Did people here do that? Invite people over for tea, the way they did in Alaska? Julie gave her a funny look and Rigel tried to be cool. "I mean, sure."

HHT

It wasn't really a house. Julie and her family lived in an apartment over the stationery store. First they went into the store, where Mrs. Han smiled at Rigel and said, "Nice to meet you." Then Julie led Rigel through the shop, through the back door marked EXIT, and up the concrete stairs to their apartment.

The Hans' living room was tidy and dim, with drawn shades and squared magazines on the coffee table. Across the narrow hall in the kitchen, the counters were crowded with canisters and jars of utensils, and the table was covered with books, papers, and cups. It was just like their table back in Alaska, and made Rigel feel at home right away. Julie yanked open the fridge and looked inside. She took out two cans and tossed one to Rigel.

"Is this okay? My mom won't buy soda or anything like that."

It was a can of green tea.

Rigel had been looking forward to the usual comforting ritual of taking down mugs and finding tea bags and waiting for a kettle to boil. Still, once she opened the can and had a sip, the tea tasted good.

Rigel said, "I've never had this kind before. In Alaska, we drink hot tea. 'Come drink tea'—that's what people say."

Julie rummaged through a cupboard. "Oh, we drink hot tea too. Cold tea. Whatever kind of tea. When we were really little, we drank barley tea, because it doesn't have any caffeine. Mom's always after me to drink more barley tea. Says it's good for your eyesight." She tapped her glasses.

"I haven't had that one yet."

"Let me know if you want to try some. We went to the Je Mart last weekend and we are fully stocked."

A tall boy with hair down to his shoulders came into the kitchen. He said to Julie, "If you're looking for the Pop-Tarts, I finished them off."

"Danny! That's so not fair!"

"You snooze, you lose." He got his own can of tea. "I'm Danny, by the way," he said to Rigel.

"I'm Rigel," she mumbled.

"He gets out of school before I do and eats up all the good snacks," Julie said to Rigel. "Ugh! Come on."

In her small bedroom, Julie got down on her belly and searched under the bed for a while before crawling back out and brandishing a box of strawberry Pop-Tarts. "I know I've got raspberry ones under here too . . ."

Rigel lay down on the rug to help search. Boxes of sweaters and coats, a few socks, a library book that Julie was happy to find, and then, at last, the second box of Pop-Tarts, behind Julie's snow boots.

They sat on the rug sneezing for a few minutes. "Which is your favorite flavor?" Julie asked Rigel.

"I've never had them."

"You're kidding! Why not?"

Probably because they were really expensive, Rigel guessed. But she didn't say it. She shrugged instead. "Maybe they didn't sell them in Fort McPhee. The store there was super small."

"You can try one of each and see which one you like better." Julie got up from the rug and gave Rigel a hand. "Your first Pop-Tart. We should mark this on a calendar and make it Pop-Tart Day. I like them toasted, so it's back out to the kitchen."

"Hey!" Danny protested as Julie pushed up beside him at the counter and put two Pop-Tarts into the toaster.

Julie tossed her hair back, the same way Hayden Foyle liked to do. "You snooze, you lose," she told Danny.

Chapter 10

There was a fancy SUV parked in front of Grandma's house. Rigel watched it as she walked down the street, comfortably full of green tea and Pop-Tarts. Inside the car, a woman in huge sunglasses spoke into a wireless headset while inspecting her nails.

Grandma's front door opened. Christian came out in sweatpants and a T-shirt. His sunglasses were mirrored, so you couldn't see his eyes, and his thick brown hair was ruffled like he'd just run his fingers through it. His usual look. He nodded curtly at Rigel, went to the SUV at the curb, and got in. It pulled away and sped off down the street.

Willow must be home.

Lately Willow was always out—club meetings, or the

coffee shop, or over at Christian's house, where he preferred to hang out because his mom bought his favorite junk food and they had a big-screen TV with the latest video games. He must like *Willow*, but he didn't seem interested in the rest of them. He never spent much time in their house and never said more than "Hey," not even to Izzy, who had done her best to wheedle something else out of him. And when he was visiting, he had a way of glancing around as if their house amused him somehow. But then, everything seemed to amuse Christian. He was like Davis Rogers that way.

Anyway, Willow liked him. Even more than she liked *him*, she liked being his girlfriend, Rigel thought. Because she was Christian's girlfriend, Willow now sat at the best lunch table with all the best people. And she had joined the SSC, the School Service Club, which included only popular girls. Rigel wasn't sure how they kept the unpopular girls out, but they did somehow. Willow said so.

Today Willow was sitting by herself with a schoolbook and a glass of milk. The kitchen was quiet and smelled like cookies baking. Grandma didn't buy sweets at the supermarket very often. If the girls wanted cookies, they baked them.

"Hi," Willow said.

"I saw Christian leave. Where was he going?"

"Doctor's appointment. He walked me home first."

"There was some lady in a fancy car picking him up."

"His mom."

Rigel went to the sink for a glass of water. Was Willow in

a good mood? The fact that she'd said "Hi" was a good sign, so Rigel decided to take a chance. "Do you think I'm rude?"

Willow tapped her pencil thoughtfully. "Who said you were rude?"

"Mrs. Green."

"Oh, her," Willow said. They all knew who Mrs. Green was. If Grandma or Lila asked Rigel what the worst part of her school day had been, Rigel's answer often involved Mrs. Green. "Did she say something dumb?"

Rigel nodded.

"Well, sometimes when someone says something dumb, you have this way of looking at them. You act like you're amazed they know how to breathe."

"I do?"

"Yes," Willow said. "You do. I can't believe you don't know that about yourself. And you need to smile more. People here smile a lot."

Rigel had noticed that too. Grin, grin, grin, all day long. She tried out a smile. "Okay."

"And make sure you always say 'please' and 'thank you' and that stuff. It's important here." Willow tapped her pencil again, then let it drop. "You want to know something?"

"What?"

"Christian told me I should quit Art Club."

Rigel halted the water glass an inch from her lips.

"See? There's the look I just told you about! You look like that's the dumbest thing you've ever heard. He says Art Club is for weirdos and rejects, and people will get the wrong idea about me."

That *was* the dumbest thing Rigel had ever heard. Willow loved Art Club. It was her favorite thing about school. She liked it even more than her table in the cafeteria.

And Willow's friends from Art Club were the nicest. They never stared at Rigel and whispered to one another, or ignored her. They smiled and said hi. And Rigel liked the way some of them dressed, like colorful birds in their best feathers. Especially Judit, Willow's best Art Club friend. You never knew what color Judit's hair was going to be from week to week.

"What are you going to do?" Rigel asked.

Willow rested her chin on her hands. "That's what I'm trying to figure out."

"I wouldn't give up Art Club if I were you."

"Rigel, you don't know what you're talking about. When you're in high school, maybe you'll get it. *Maybe*."

If this was what having a boyfriend was like, Rigel was glad she didn't have one.

She wouldn't have minded having a friend, though. She envied Willow those. Rigel just needed one friend for the one year she had to get through in Connecticut.

After today, though, maybe she had it. Going home with Julie had been a good start, anyway.

The oven bell dinged, and Willow got up to take out the cookies.

The phone rang.

"Rye Bear!" Willow said. "You pick that up."

Rigel usually walked away from ringing phones. She hated the noise, and trying to talk to someone she couldn't see, and the phone was always for someone else anyway. But today Rigel was glad she answered.

"Hey!" came Bear's familiar deep voice. "There's my Rye girl!"

Rigel practically shouted out her "Hi!" She covered the receiver and said to Willow, "It's Bear!"

Willow screwed up her mouth, shrugged, and went back to her cookies.

"I've been thinking about you," Rigel said. "Where are you now?"

"In Fort McPhee. I just finished my two weeks on and figured I'd stop in and get the mail. Sophie says hi."

"Tell her hi from me. And tell Kimora hi too." Rigel took the warm cookie Willow handed her and nodded thanks. "I wish I was there."

"Connecticut's that good, huh? Liking school any better?"

"Nope."

Bear laughed. "Making any friends?"

Rigel thought of Julie. She wasn't sure whether she could call her a friend yet. "I don't know. It doesn't matter anyway," she said, being careful, because Willow was only a few feet away, scooping a second round of cookie dough onto the baking sheets.

Bear knew what she meant without any need to spell it out. "Yeah, it really doesn't," he agreed. "Not for just the one year. Rye Bear, if your sisters are around, can you put them on? I hate to rush, but someone asked me over to eat and I want to grab a shower at the laundromat first."

Must be someone important for Bear to take a shower in the middle of the day, when he wasn't even done sweating. Rigel waved at Willow and held up the receiver.

"I love those letters you're sending me. Keep them coming, okay?" Bear added quickly.

"I love you." Rigel held out the receiver for Willow to take. She regretted giving up the phone the moment she'd done it. It was always like that when Bear called. Rigel was never done telling him everything she wanted him to know.

HHT

Countdown day 287. Mid-October, and more than 20 percent through Rigel's Connecticut year.

Rigel did some calculations standing in the noisy hallway next to Julie's locker.

21.3 percent, to be exact.

"You want to go to the movies this weekend?" Julie asked before dropping one of her gym shoes. Rigel chased it into the middle of the hall and grabbed it out from under the feet of an eighth grader, who clicked her tongue in annoyance. Julie smiled in thanks, threw the shoe into her locker, and banged its door shut.

"Sure. Which one?"

"I'll check the listings."

Connecticut could never be as good as Alaska. That was settled, as far as Rigel was concerned. But there were things about it that weren't so bad.

Like comfy movie theaters you could walk to that sold soda and popcorn and had a choice of movies to see (unlike the Fort McPhee community center, where people sat on folding chairs and either saw the one film showing or didn't see anything at all).

Like ice cream parlors with dozens of flavors.

Like having friends who only lived a few blocks away instead of miles.

Rigel and Julie had been to the movies twice. They had eaten dinner at each other's houses. They walked home from school together, helped each other out with homework, and called each other up to talk (because neither one had a cell phone to text with). Rigel was pretty sure they were friends.

Although she knew better than to ask. That would be weird.

Having a friend in Connecticut made a big difference.

They passed by the lobby bulletin board, where the populars liked to hang out for some reason. Hayden, Celeste, and

Marion were there so often that some kids called them the "bulletin board girls."

"Rigel," someone said.

Uh-oh. Rigel walked faster, pretending she hadn't heard.

"*Harman!* Are you deaf or something? Come here."

Hayden, Celeste, and Marion stood with Davis and Jake and other kids Rigel didn't know. The girls all had their hairbrushes out. They were always doing stuff to their hair—brushing it, twisting it, putting barrettes in, taking them back out . . .

"We want to see how long your hair is," Hayden said.

"I'm pretty sure it's longer than mine," Marion said.

"No way!" Celeste shouted. "Yours is totally longer."

"Take it out and let us see."

Rigel reluctantly pulled the hair band out and pushed her hands through her hair. It spilled away from her fingers and fell down her back.

"Oh my God, it's soooo long." Marion sighed, like Rigel had done something really special by growing out her hair.

"How did you grow it out that long?" one girl asked—a girl whose name Rigel didn't know. "What conditioner do you use?"

"Conditioner? Please!" Celeste grabbed a handful, like Rigel's hair was something she was thinking about buying at a store. "Her hair is totally dry. Marion's hair is in much better shape."

"Come on, be fair. Rigel's hair is beautiful," Marion said.

Rigel's heart rose. No one had ever called anything about her "beautiful" before.

"Um, hello? Hayden's hair is *so* much prettier," Celeste said.

Hayden slapped Celeste on the arm. "No, it's not! I *hate* the color. It's such a boring brown!"

They were the ones who were boring.

Rigel could never think of anything to say to them.

Anyway, they seemed to be done inspecting her, so she swept her hair forward over her shoulder and started the familiar braid.

"Stop!" Hayden said, like this was an emergency. "Leave it down! It's totally cuter like that."

"Leave it down," Marion ordered.

"It's better that way," said another girl. "When you have it in that braid, you look like someone on the History Channel."

"I know, right?" Julie said, out of nowhere. "I keep telling her that."

Rigel gave Julie a glance. Hair was not something they talked about. But Julie ignored the look, and her bright smile made Rigel remember Willow's advice about how to get along with the right people. *Just smile a lot.*

Sam, Sylvie, and Corey passed by, headed for homeroom. Those three always seemed to be together.

"Sam! Hey, Sam!" Celeste said.

Sam's head dipped a little and he walked faster.

"Dino!" Davis called. "Stop pretending you can't hear us!"

Sam stopped and turned. Corey and Sylvie stopped too and stood behind Sam, and the way they stayed there made Rigel understand what people meant when they said someone "had their back."

"The cafeteria"—Celeste pointed dramatically—"is *that* way."

It was one of the fat jokes they threw at Sam all the time. Laughter started percolating. Maybe it had been a little funny, one time, but come on. So what if Sam was fat? He was nice to everyone, even the kids who were mean to him. Just a few days ago, he had lent Rigel a pencil and told her to keep it.

Sam sounded tired. "I knew that, actually."

"Oh. I thought you might have missed breakfast," Hayden said sweetly.

"Or second breakfast!" Jake shouted.

Like Jake was one to talk. He wasn't exactly skinny himself. Bulletin board laughter rang out. Julie laughed too.

"Yeah, all right. Amuse yourselves." Sam turned away.

The bell rang and Rigel trailed along behind the bulletin board kids to class.

####

That stupid loose hair was in her way all morning. It got into her mouth, it fell over her notebook when she was taking notes, it got caught in a screw in her desk during science class and had to be yanked free, and by lunch it was so tangled that it took ages for Rigel to comb it out and get it in a braid again.

Julie and Rigel walked home from school with Rigel's hair thumping across her back in the familiar braid.

Julie walked faster than usual and said less than usual. Rigel was pretty sure Julie was annoyed about something, but she wasn't sure how to ask.

"Why are you wearing that braid again?" Julie asked. "Didn't you hear what Hayden said about your hair? You should totally start wearing it like that."

"No way. It would make me crazy. Willow spends about two hours a day brushing hers."

"Yeah, but everyone's wearing their hair loose like that this year. I wish my mom would let me grow mine out." Julie tugged on her hair, like that would make it grow faster. "'Too much trouble,'" she added, in her mom's voice.

"It is too much trouble, unless you're wearing it braided."

"Well, okay, but Hayden's not going to like it."

"Why would she care?"

Julie ignored this question. "If Hayden told me my hair looked good that way, I would totally wear it down."

"You would?"

"Of course!" For some reason, the silence that fell was an awkward one. Then Julie said, "Rigel? I hope you don't mind me saying this, but . . ."

What was Julie being shy about? She usually spoke her mind straight out.

"Did you know that sometimes you wear the same shirt two days in a row?"

"Only if it's still clean."

Another pause stretched out like a piece of chewing gum.

"Is that a problem?" Rigel asked.

"Well, it's weird. Don't you think? No one else does it." Julie swung her arms with vigor. "I mean, even I don't have to do that, and my mom thinks two pairs of jeans are enough for the whole school year."

"I don't have to. Lila and Grandma are always talking about taking me shopping. They wanted to take me before school started, but I wouldn't."

"Why not?"

Because the mall was noisy, and it was crowded, and everything seemed so expensive compared to what Lila earned. The mannequins were totally creepy, like ginormous Barbie dolls. And Rigel wouldn't be able to wear any of those clothes when she went back home to Alaska anyway. Rigel had a feeling Julie wouldn't understand any of that, so she said nothing.

Finally, Julie shrugged. "Well, anyway, it was smart of you to wait. Now you know what everyone is wearing, and you can buy the right stuff. Get Willow to go with you; she always looks good."

Did Rigel really have to brave the mall and waste Lila's money just to make some snotty girls like her? "I don't really need anything," she mumbled.

Julie stopped short. "You know, I don't get you sometimes. It's kind of a big deal, Hayden saying you have pretty hair. Don't you want to be popular? It's a lot better than being a loser."

Was Julie calling Rigel a loser, or saying both of them were losers? Neither one was a good thing.

They stood at a red light without looking at each other.

"I'm not a loser," Rigel said at last.

"Yes, you are! We both are. I can't believe you don't even know that."

They didn't have much else to say for the rest of their walk home.

HHT

It rained all weekend. Even Rigel didn't want to go outside.

Maybe that was why Julie didn't call about the movies after all. When Rigel tried calling her, Danny said Julie wasn't home. Maybe they were having a busy weekend in the shop and Julie was helping out downstairs.

Maybe.

HHT

Countdown day 280. Thursday evening, right before supper.

Going upstairs, Rigel heard voices coming from inside Willow's room.

"Those two reds just don't go together."

"But too much blue is boring. What if we moved this one over here? That works, I think."

Rigel knocked at Willow's door. Willow and Judit looked up from the pictures and cloth scraps spread out over Willow's desk.

"What's up, bae?" Judit's hair was streaked with purple this week.

"Grandma said supper will be ready in a few minutes, and"—Rigel swallowed before saying what she had rehearsed—"Judit is welcome to stay." She couldn't help it, she still felt shy around strangers.

Willow said to Judit, "Want to eat with us? We could work on this some more after dinner."

"I wish I could, but Mom's got class. I have to babysit Thing One and Thing Two." That was what Judit called her little brothers. She picked up her backpack. "Maybe we can look at it after school tomorrow?"

"I've got SSC then."

"Boring. I don't know how you stay awake in those meetings!"

Willow smiled. "Sometimes I don't," she whispered.

"Ha! Okay, I have to go. Text me later. See you, Rigel!"

"Bye," Rigel said, and listened to the jingle of Judit's backpack going away down the hall. "What are you working on?" Rigel asked Willow, who was bent over the pictures again, frowning.

"We're doing some collages for art class. Kind of middle school, but, you know, it's an assignment. Do you need something? I'm actually trying to concentrate here."

Willow sure loved having her own room now. The way she acted, no one would ever guess that she'd once shared a bedroom with two sisters.

"Can I ask you something real quick? It's about Julie."

"Your friend Julie? What about her?"

Rigel came inside Willow's room and closed the door. "I think she's mad at me, or something."

"Did she say she was mad?"

"No. She ignores me."

"Ignores you like you're not even there?"

Rigel nodded. "Like we don't know each other."

Willow looked up from the collage. "For how long?"

"Four days if you just count school days, six days if you count last weekend."

"And you've tried to talk to her?"

"I asked her whether she was mad at me. She acted like she didn't understand why I was asking."

"Did you do something to her?"

"No! I mean . . . Not to her. There was this one dumb thing in the hallway, with the bulletin board girls. They wanted me to take my hair out, and then they all said it was pretty, and I should wear it down. Julie said I should too, but—"

"See? I told you that exact same thing!"

"I know, but anyway," Rigel said, squirming, "then Julie said I should buy some new clothes and stuff, and I shouldn't wear the same shirt two days in a row."

"You know Grandma and Lila would take you shopping if you wanted, right? They took Izzy and me."

"But I don't want new clothes. I like these clothes." Rigel had enough new stuff going on in her life without bagfuls of weird, stiff clothes that smelled funny. Still, she thought the idea over. "I guess I could try that," she admitted.

Willow sat on her bed, patting the space beside her. Rigel sat down too.

"I think you've been dumped," Willow said.

"Oh."

Rigel wasn't totally clueless. She knew what being dumped meant. Some of the girls in Fort McPhee fought with each other. They argued, stopped talking, made up again . . . Girls did that everywhere, Lila said.

"It happens a lot in middle school," Willow said. "I read something on *Teen Vogue* about it."

"Should I try to talk to her again?"

Willow shook her head. "No point. That would just be embarrassing."

"Has anyone ever dumped you?"

"Not yet." Willow looked sad for a moment, before she shook it off and went back to her advice. "Join a club or something. That's what the article said to do. It'll help you meet new people. You're not totally hopeless, you know." Willow smiled so Rigel would know she was joking. "You can make other friends."

Ugh, no.

She should have followed her dad's advice right from the start: kept her head down, done her chores, and waited for the year to be over. No point in wasting her energy on these Connecticut kids. She'd never understand them in a million years, let alone one. Better just focus on getting through the next 280 days before she could get out of here and never come back.

Chapter 11

ountdown day 262.

The maple trees outside the school library were almost bare. The leaves had been moved into piles by leaf blowers—which for small machines gave off giant amounts of stink and noise—and taken away somewhere. The last few leaves still rattling on the branches were a dull brown. The grass was getting brown to match.

It was November in Connecticut.

In Fort McPhee, there was snow on the ground. Kimora had said so. Rigel wished she were back in Alaska right now, splitting and stacking wood, sorting through their canned goods, mending socks and mittens—doing everything bush Alaskans do to get ready for the cold season.

"Here are your books, Rigel." Mrs. Leibmann pushed *Gifts of the Crow* and *Crow Planet* across the counter. "Now, take good care of those. Don't get me in trouble with the lending library. They're due in two weeks."

"Thank you, Mrs. Leibmann." It was easy to remember to be polite to Mrs. Leibmann. She was so nice, she never made Rigel nervous.

"Are you doing a research paper on crows?"

"Just trying to find out more about them."

The heat came on with its usual noisy whoosh and filled the room with the smell of toasted air.

Julie came into the library. She walked to the counter and shoved a few books into the return bin. She had a frown on her face, like she was worried about something. But Rigel wasn't going to know what, because nowadays Julie ignored Rigel and Rigel returned the favor. No one would have guessed they'd ever sat next to each other in the movies, sharing candy.

Rigel sat down at a computer and logged into her email. Hayden, Celeste, and Marion inspected her from their table near the printer.

"I like your shirt, Rigel." Marion nudged Hayden and grinned.

Rigel glanced down at herself. She was wearing a red flannel hoodie Lila had bought her at the mall. Even Willow had said it was cute.

She should have known changing clothes wouldn't make

a difference. Once Hayden decided she had it in for someone, she wasn't changing her mind over a few extra shirts.

Celeste said, "I can't believe Rigel's wearing a new top. I guess someone had a yard sale last weekend."

"Or she went dumpster diving," Hayden said in the sweet voice she reserved for remarks like that.

Mrs. Leibmann shushed them.

Corey, Sylvie, and Sam, who were sharing a table by the window with books spread out all around them, put their heads together to whisper. Sylvie wrinkled her nose sympathetically and gave Rigel a quick wave that might have meant *Don't let them get to you*, or even *Come over here and sit with us*. But Rigel didn't waste too much time pondering it.

She logged out of the computer, got up, and slung her backpack on. She owed Kimora an email, but she'd just have to write it later.

At least it was lunchtime. This was the one time of day when she could get away from the bulletin board girls. Away from Julie. Away from all of them.

Outside, she sat down on the edge of the old patio and opened her lunch box.

One good thing about not eating in the cafeteria was that Rigel didn't have to wonder what anyone thought of her food anymore. She could eat sardine sandwiches whenever she wanted. And that's what she had today, plus a thermos of milk, celery sticks, some blueberries, a hard-boiled egg, and her last piece of salmon jerky.

She chewed it slowly. No one could say she hadn't made that one bag last a long time. 103 days to be exact.

Maybe Bear would send more for Christmas.

The crow came hopping across the grass to see what she was up to. Crows were curious birds, the same way ravens were. It was still wary around her, but not like it had been a month ago. Rigel and it had been sharing this space for weeks now, and Rigel had never done anything to startle or scare it.

You couldn't say the crow was flourishing, although its eyes were still bright. It looked dirty and untidy, its feathers sticking out any old way. Maybe the dumpster pickings were slim lately.

She shoved the garbage from her lunch back into her lunch box. There were a few blueberries that had gone soft, and she tossed them out into the grass.

The crow hopped over nimbly and gobbled them down.

It turned its head to study Rigel. It didn't glance away for a moment. The bird didn't trust her, but it was hoping for more food.

Rigel looked down at the hard-boiled egg in her hand.

Bear and Lila had always been strict about them not feeding wild creatures. Feeding seemed like the right thing to do, but it usually wasn't. Leaving animal remains was okay, because birds and animals always fed on carrion when they could find it. But putting out food? It wasn't a good idea. Bear and Lila agreed on that, even when they had stopped agreeing on anything else.

Animals are tough and they're well evolved, Lila said. They can survive, and when they don't, that's part of the natural cycle. It drives evolution.

Bear put it more simply. You shouldn't turn a wild animal into a pet.

But the bird waited with its bright button eye turned in her direction. It didn't beg, but it waited.

If it was eating out of a dumpster, a little egg couldn't hurt.

Rigel gently tossed the egg out into the grass.

The crow cocked its head. It was waiting for her to leave. It didn't want to get close to her. That was a good thing. Crows were smart.

Rigel got up, slung on her backpack, and brushed the seat of her pants. "Enjoy," she said.

IHHT

Countdown day 261. Rigel discovered the crow liked sardines just as much as she did.

IHHT

Countdown day 260. The crow also liked cold pizza. It ate so much of Rigel's lunch that she had to stop in the cafeteria for some chicken nuggets before going to class. It was an act of desperation, because Rigel thought chicken nuggets were the grossest food ever.

HHt

Countdown day 259.

The school buses had gone a while ago, and Rigel and Mrs. Leibmann were the only two left in the library. Mrs. Leibmann was tidying up and said Rigel could stay until she was finished.

Rigel had a few printouts, still warm from the printer, beside her on the table. She clicked the link to one last article and read it carefully.

Crows are omnivorous and always seem hungry. Much like teenagers, they are not picky eaters and enjoy junk food. While there's nothing wrong with a few Doritos now and then, healthier options for the birds include meat scraps, cheese, hard-boiled eggs (no need to peel), and sunflower seeds and peanuts in the shell. Another good option can be pet food. Dry cat or dog kibble in small chunks is cheap, keeps well, and supplies complete nutrition.

She clicked PRINT and got up to get the article from the printer.

"I'm ready to leave, Rigel. Are you about done?"

Rigel nodded, stuffing the printouts into her backpack.

"How is your research coming along?" Mrs. Leibmann tapped some papers into a stack.

Rigel hesitated. "It's not really research. I mean, not for school or anything." She was sure she sounded like an idiot. She didn't fit in here, no matter how hard she tried. "It's just something I need to know more about."

"I see. Personal enrichment." The librarian nodded. "Even better."

When Mrs. Leibmann put it that way, Rigel's research sounded pretty good, actually.

"See you tomorrow." Rigel waved goodbye and walked out the door.

On her way home, she stopped by the pet store downtown and bought a plastic container of dog food.

If she was going to feed that crow, she might as well feed it something that was good for it.

HHT

Countdown day 252. 30.9 percent of the way through Rigel's Connecticut year.

Call it 31 percent and be done with it, Rigel decided.

She was feeling relaxed, because countdown day 252 was Thanksgiving. And Thanksgiving meant four days off from school.

The smell of roasting turkey drifted out of the kitchen and a fire crackled in the fireplace.

There was only one issue to disturb Rigel's peace.

The crow.

School was out for a long weekend. That meant four days without fresh trash in the dumpster and without Rigel's dog food supplements. And what if someone decided to make sure the dumpster lid was tightly shut before the long vacation?

Four days was a long time for a crow.

Rigel put down the copy of *Flatland* that Mr. Trayvick had lent her. She'd better go by school and make sure that dumb bird was all right.

Rigel went into the kitchen, found one of the bread bags Grandma saved for reuse, and raided the fridge for a few things. She tied the bread bag, put it in the pocket of her jacket, and then stopped back by the living room, where everyone was comfortable.

"I thought I might take a walk," Rigel said.

Lila looked up from her *New Yorker*. "We could all take a walk."

"I'm cozy." Izzy was lying in the best spot in the living room, right in front of the fire.

"So am I," Lila confessed.

Willow flipped her *Vogue* shut. "I'll go." She must have seen a funny look on Rigel's face. "If that's okay."

Rigel said, "Sure, it's okay," not fooling Willow one bit, she could tell.

Outside, Willow said, "Want to walk over to the Lee Price Chappell Wilderness and see if there's any action going on? Maybe two squirrels are having a fight over a black walnut or something."

"I need to go by school first."

"You don't like going there even when it's open. Why are we going there today?"

"I just have to do something." Rigel hoped Willow wouldn't press.

But as they walked along, Willow kept shooting off one annoying question after another.

"What's the big secret?"

"Come on, Rigel! Just tell me!"

"You're so weird lately. You've always been weird, but now you're weird about everything."

"I know, you have a boyfriend. Tell me about him. Is he cute?"

They were finally in front of the middle school. In desperation, Rigel said, "If you wait out front here and stop asking questions, I'll do your share of the dishes tonight."

Willow tilted her head, considering this offer. Then she sat down on the bench Rigel indicated.

"Fine. But if you take too long all bets are off. It's freezing." Willow took out her phone and bent over it so her long hair swept forward and hid her face.

Rigel went around back, whistling as she went.

The lid of the dumpster was slightly open as always, and judging from the reek, there was plenty of garbage left inside. She felt silly for worrying.

The crow had heard her whistle. It was pacing around in front of the back stoop. It came toward her, cawing softly.

"Hello there." She undid the bread bag and laid out her offerings.

She had foraged a leftover chicken thigh, a double-handful of blueberries, and—because it was Thanksgiving—several cubes of cheese. The crow liked cheese.

"Enjoy," she said, like she always did.

The crow started in on the cheese while she sat and watched it, her arms folded against the chill. She hadn't worn a coat. It was a point of pride with Rigel that she didn't need more than a jacket in Connecticut.

The crow finished up the last cheese cube and turned its head to look at her. It hopped closer. What was it doing?

Closer again.

Rigel sat absolutely still. As usual when she did that, her nose itched like mad and all she could think about was scratching it, but she didn't move anything other than her eyes. She didn't even twitch a finger.

The bird was close enough now for her to touch it. It kept its gaze on her, but it didn't move back.

As slowly as she could, Rigel raised her hand.

The crow stayed put.

Rigel reached out and touched its head.

The crow didn't move.

Heart beating quickly, Rigel gently scratched the crow above one eye.

The crow grabbed her finger in its bill. It wasn't a snap or peck. It held Rigel's finger firmly and made a noise she hadn't heard from it before. Almost a humming noise: *Mmm-mmm.*

Rigel did her best to make the same noise back. The crow looked at her with what Rigel thought was disdain. Apparently, she had gotten the sounds all wrong. It let go of her finger and hopped back to deal with the blueberries.

Rigel was asking herself whether touching the crow had actually happened when the crow gave a quick *Caw-caw-caw* and flapped away quickly into the closest tree.

It was flying better now.

"What's the matter?" Rigel looked around to see what had startled it.

Willow stood at the corner of the building, hands in her pockets, watching.

"Hey! We had a deal."

"I decided I didn't mind doing a few dishes. Are you feeding that crow?"

"Just stay over there. I don't want it to get used to people."

"Then maybe you shouldn't be feeding it."

The crow cocked its head, sizing up the situation. It eyed Willow, then Rigel, then Willow again. Taking a chance, it flapped back down onto the grass, seized the chicken, and dragged it backward toward the dumpster. It tore a big chunk of meat loose.

"I wonder where its family is," Willow said. "I'm pretty sure crows hang in groups."

From her books, Rigel knew Willow was right. Still, she said, "Ravens don't always."

Willow gave a low laugh. "That's no raven. Not unless someone pocket-sized it for the suburbs. Do you mind if I sketch it?"

"Does Christian let you do that anymore?"

"Oh, shut up."

"You owe me a dollar."

"Not if Lila didn't hear me." Willow took the small sketch pad from her pocket. She usually carried one now.

"He tried to make you quit Art Club!"

"We talked about it and worked it out. When you're more mature, you'll get it." She flipped open the pad cover. "What's the bird's name?"

"It doesn't have a name."

"You're feeding it every day and it doesn't have a name?"

"I didn't think it needed one." Rigel studied the crow, who had gone back to its favorite, the blueberries. One by one, it snapped them up. "Blueberry," she said, before Willow could suggest some dumb human name that had nothing to do with a wild animal. "Its name is Blueberry."

"Blueberry." Willow's pencil swished over the paper as she drew.

"Hey, Willow? Do me a favor? Promise not to tell Lila about it."

"It's just a crow that you feed now and then. Why can't Lila know?"

Rigel shrugged. It wasn't just Lila. She didn't want any grown-ups to know. She hadn't even told Bear.

Willow flipped a page and started another sketch. "Just let me do one more before we head back . . ." Willow's pencil moved quickly over the pad. She couldn't really talk and sketch at the same time.

Blueberry found a leftover cube of cheese in the grass. This time it stayed close. It was getting used to them.

IHT

"How was your walk?" Lila asked at Thanksgiving dinner. "Did you see anything interesting?"

"I got to see Rigel's crow." Willow poured gravy over her turkey.

Rigel sat without moving, gripping her fork and knife tightly. Willow was such a *rat*.

"Crow?" Lila asked. "What crow?"

"What crow? That crow from way back on the first day of school?" Grandma was interested in everything, the same way Izzy always was. "The one with the white markings?"

Willow shot Rigel a pert look, like she had been cute, and helped herself to another slice of turkey.

Rigel stuffed a Parker House roll into her mouth and chewed, hoping they would move on to something else. But Grandma and Lila waited her out. They really wanted to know.

"It's no big deal," Rigel said at last. "The crow's hanging

around the back of school nowadays. I give it something now and then, so it has something to eat besides stuff from the dumpster."

Lila nodded. "That's probably why it's staying around. A steady supply of food."

"Rigel calls it Blueberry." Willow smiled. Any more cheerful and Rigel would kick her under the table.

"That's cute," Izzy said. Since starting kindergarten, "cute" was Izzy's favorite word of praise.

"It likes blueberries," Rigel said.

"Just like ravens," Lila remarked. In the Bush, ravens picked blueberries the same way people did. "How about the rest of its family? Do you ever see them?"

Rigel shook her head. "It's alone."

"That's strange. Crows are usually social, the way people are. When a baby crow matures, a lot of times it stays with its parents for a few years and helps them raise chicks. They hang out in groups, and usually in the winter they all roost together. Warmer and safer that way, easier to protect themselves."

Rigel knew crows were different from ravens that way. Young ravens tended to go through a rowdy phase, the way some teenagers did. They gathered in noisy groups and did dumb stuff. They didn't hang around and help their parents with the younger siblings, the way crows often did.

But she had never seen another crow hanging around Blueberry.

Blueberry was alone, the same way she was.

"I wonder what happened to its family," Willow said.

"Probably its parents got divorced." Rigel stabbed a fork down into her sweet potato casserole.

⊞⊦⊦

There was an order to doing dishes the right way while using the smallest amount of water.

First the glasses got washed, then the silverware, then the plates and bowls, and lastly the greasy pans. Rigel could get almost a kitchenful of dishes done with one sink of water if she was careful.

She didn't want to get into bad habits. This time next year she'd be packing water again, unless Bear got around to installing that pump system he talked about sometimes.

Willow picked up the dish towel Rigel had left ready and wiped a water glass dry.

"What are you doing here?" Rigel asked.

"I didn't wait for you out front, so I have to help after all."

"Go away. I'll do them by myself."

"Oh, come on. You're such a baby sometimes." Willow put the glass on the draining board.

"I'd rather be a baby than a snitch."

"I didn't promise not to tell."

"You knew I didn't want Lila to know."

"Why can't she know about Blueberry? Why does it have to be such a secret?"

Because secrets were sticky. That was why. If Rigel started telling people her little secrets it would be too easy to let the biggest one slip: her return to Alaska. But she couldn't say anything about that to Willow. "I didn't feel like hearing a lecture about feeding Blueberry." After all, that was true too.

"She didn't lecture you."

Rigel ignored this, handing Willow a plate.

"You know, I don't think it's really fair how you're punishing Lila for everything that happened," Willow remarked.

"I'm not *punishing* her."

"Meanwhile, Bear gets off scot-free for all of it. Don't you think he had a little itsy-bitsy *something* to do with the fact that we ended up here?"

"It wasn't his idea," Rigel said.

"Yeah? Well, he sure didn't have a better one. I didn't hear him suggest any great plan to help us stay in Alaska."

That's all you know, Rigel wanted to say. *Bear has a plan. But it's just for me. I'm going back and you're going to be stuck here.* But she couldn't say anything.

That stupid promise again!

Chapter 12

ountdown day 223.

That number should have made Rigel feel good. 223 was a prime, and she felt lucky on prime days. Even more important, 223 marked the last day of school before their winter break.

It also meant that she was 38.9 percent (okay, call it 39 percent) of the way through this year.

But all Rigel could think about were the presents on the other kids' desks.

It was almost Christmas, and it turned out that kids in Connecticut swapped presents on the last day before winter break. Rigel hadn't known. There hadn't been an announcement.

Even if she had known, it wouldn't have mattered. She didn't have any friends here. Except for Blueberry.

Almost every other kid in homeroom had something, even if it was just a holiday card in a bright red or blue envelope. Some had way more. Hayden's desk had a stack. Rigel's desk was empty. She tried telling herself it didn't matter, but it did. She wiped her nose and hoped no one else could tell.

Mrs. Green came in wearing one of her Christmas sweaters. She slapped her folders down. "The School Handbook—"

"—the School Handbook—" Jake mocked.

"The School Handbook specifies that students may not exchange holiday gifts in class unless an official gift exchange was announced. I did not announce a gift exchange."

The chatter in the classroom died away.

"Now I'm going to clean off this whiteboard. And any gifts left out when I turn back around are getting confiscated immediately."

She picked up the eraser.

All around Rigel, kids scrambled to stuff gifts into their backpacks and bags. Rigel smiled down at the top of her desk. Sometimes Mrs. Green wasn't so bad after all.

"That's better," Mrs. Green said, putting down the eraser and going over to her desk. She pulled out her chair, sat down, then jumped up again. She held up a present that must have been left on her chair. Not too big, not too small, and wrapped in shiny blue-and-silver paper, with matching silver ribbon and a fancy bow that was now flattened by Mrs. Green's rear end. It was the kind of bow that Rigel's family put into a box after Christmas to use again.

Rigel wondered who liked Mrs. Green enough to give her a gift like that.

Mrs. Green looked at the card under the ribbon. "This is for Rigel Harman."

A scornful snort came from Hayden's side of the room.

"Well, Rigel, this is against school rules, but you can come and get your gift, provided you put it away immediately."

It was embarrassing having to go up and take the gift from Mrs. Green. Mrs. Green smiled at Rigel, which didn't happen very often, and there was lipstick on one of her front teeth.

At the same time, it felt great to have a present like every other kid in class.

Sam leaned out from his desk to get a better look at the pretty wrapping paper, then gave Rigel a quick thumbs-up.

Mrs. Green shushed the class again, and announcements started.

Rigel slid the gift into her backpack, its blue-and-silver paper glittering. This present must be from someone in homeroom. But she couldn't imagine who would give her anything. Julie looked as surprised as everyone else. One thing was for sure, Hayden didn't like it one bit. She was glaring across the room, like Rigel had taken something that really belonged to her.

HHT

School was finally over for winter break.

Rigel sat down on the back stoop and gave Blueberry the chunk of banana muffin she had saved for it. From out front drifted the noisy commotion of the afternoon buses being boarded. No one was going to come back here. She was safe.

She took the present out of her backpack.

Blueberry abandoned the muffin and hopped closer to investigate.

The card under the ribbon showed a gray rabbit sitting up in the snow with a golden star in its paws. *Peace Throughout the Year* it said inside, and underneath someone had printed:

> *Rigel, don't let Them catch you reading This.*
> *Happy holidays,*
> *Your Friends*
> *P.S. And don't shoot this bunny. Okay?*

She carefully opened the fancy wrapping paper. There was a book inside. Not a broken-back yard sale special or a library book in a sticky plastic cover, but a brand-new paperback that smelled good, like a bookstore. *The Hitchhiker's Guide to the Galaxy* by someone named Douglas Adams.

It had the number 42 on the cover.

Was it a math book? Could it be from Mr. Trayvick? He was always lending her math books. But no, he would have signed the card, and how would he have known that she had talked about hunting rabbits that first day in homeroom?

Anyway, it wasn't a math book—it looked more like science fiction.

"Bluebs, guess what?"

Blueberry caught her eye.

"Someone likes me." She looked at the card again. "More than one person. At least two people like me. But who?"

Blueberry gave a low rattle in its throat, the way one crow chats to its friend. *Kr-rrr.*

"Besides you, I mean." Rigel reached out and gave Blueberry a scratch on its head. "I just wish I knew who they were."

She riffled through the book to enjoy its new-paper smell. Then she spied a quick flash in the grass. The crow was sneaking away with the silver ribbon.

"Blueberry, bring that back."

Blueberry squawked and nipped at her hand.

"You stop that. We're going to share this."

Blueberry liked shiny things. It had a stash of treasures cached in different places. Rigel gave it presents sometimes. A piece of aluminum foil. A bottle cap. Blueberry's absolute favorite, a brand-new, shiny quarter.

Rigel pulled off the big fancy bow to save and let Blueberry carry away the rest.

The crow hopped away proudly. This ribbon was a real prize, even for a bird that had a quarter of its own.

HHT

Countdown day 219.

219 was not a prime, nor was it in the Fibonacci sequence, nor was it a square-free number or any other of the number types that Rigel was learning about now, thanks to Mr. Trayvick and the books he lent her.

But at least 219 was Christmas.

There was a tangle of paper and ribbons all around the tree. Not only had they gotten good presents from Lila and Grandma, Bear had sent Christmas cards with money inside.

Sorry I haven't been calling and writing more, he wrote on Rigel's. *I'm so beat at the end of the day all I'm good for is a shower, some chow, and racking out. Hang tight, kiddo! Love, Bear.*

Rigel reread the card before putting it carefully away. It was a nice card, but she wished Bear had let her know he remembered their deal.

He had probably written it when he was really tired.

"Here you go, Rye Bear." Willow handed her present over. It was long and thin—the shape of a rolled poster. Squashy on the outside and hard in the middle. Rigel had to unwrap it and then unroll it.

It was a picture of their place in Alaska, made from cloth and yarn.

The sky was blue calico and the creek at the bottom was a piece of silvery-blue lamé, stitched up to be all crinkly and look like water in motion. There were shrubs and trees sewn into place, and a cabin and outbuildings made of brown, red, and gray cloth. There were little embroidered silver fish jumping out of the lamé creek, and an embroidered raven perched on top of the smokehouse, its bright eye made from a tiny black button.

And there were people in the picture too. They were all there. Izzy sat on the cabin step wearing her red jacket and looking at a book. There was Rigel, with long brown braids and a bucket, and Willow and Lila hanging up wash—little pieces of fabric from Grandma's scraps, cut into the shapes of clothes.

Bear, with a big yellow beard made out of unraveled yellow yarn, stood down by the creek, holding an ax.

The picture even had a dowel sewn onto its back with picture wire attached. Rigel could go straight upstairs and hang it. Willow had thought of everything.

Rigel jumped on Willow and hugged her as tight as she could. "Thank you thank you thank you," she said.

"Now you can stop complaining about missing Alaska," Willow teased.

"It's true." Lila admired the picture's little details. "It's all here for you, Rye Bear."

Rigel wouldn't go that far. But it was a great present. It brought Alaska so close she could practically reach out and touch it. It would help keep her going until next summer, when she could finally go back.

HHT

Grandma glanced up from the jigsaw puzzle she was doing with Lila. "It's about time to get ready for bed, Izzy."

Christmas dinner was over, the dishes were done, and they were all relaxing.

Izzy ignored Grandma. She flipped to a new page in her coloring book and picked out a different crayon. That wasn't like Izzy. She tore through her days so fast she fell into bed willingly at night.

"What are you waiting for, Iz?" Willow asked. "Do you think Santa's going to come back and give you another present?"

"I'm waiting for Bear," Izzy said.

The Christmas music still played. The fire still snapped in the fireplace. The lights still twinkled on the tree. So why was the room suddenly quieter and darker?

"He's going to call," Izzy said. "Because it's Christmas."

Willow's lips went tight. *Did* you *tell her that?* she telegraphed across the room at Rigel with her eyebrows.

Rigel scowled back. *It wasn't me!*

"Jazmin's daddy is calling her," Izzy explained. "That means Bear is calling me." Jazmin was Izzy's best friend, and her dad was stationed in Korea.

Honestly, Rigel knew how her sister felt. All that day, there had been a part of her listening for the phone to ring. But Bear hadn't called.

"I'm going to tell him Merry Christmas." Izzy's nose was turning pink and her lips trembled, the way they did when she was getting upset.

Lila pinched her nose. Willow had her mouth open, but nothing was coming out.

"Izzy," Rigel said. "You know Bear might be working today, right?"

"Nuh-uh," Izzy said. "It's Christmas!"

"But some people work on Christmas." Rigel did her best to sound patient, like Lila. "Like doctors and nurses and firemen. And roustabouts. The Slope never shuts down, you know."

"That's true, Izzy," Lila said. "They never stop pumping the oil, because it's too hard to get it started again."

Willow threw down her magazine. "Why can't we call *him*? Lila, you must have his number."

Lila hesitated. "Okay, we can try."

They tried the number she had. No one answered. But there was voicemail, and they could leave messages. Rigel went last. She had just said, "Merry Christmas—" when a computerized voice interrupted her.

It said, *"Thank you for your message. This mailbox is now full. Your call will be returned shortly."*

Chapter 13

Countdown day 208. A boring number for the first boring day back from vacation.

"Did you have a good break?" Corey asked Rigel in homeroom.

"Yeah, it was nice." Rigel tried to think of something more exciting to say. "How about you? Did you get any good stuff?"

"Pretty good. I got some games for my Nintendo, and a gift card from my dad, and clothes, and some stuff for my millipede—"

Millipede? Maybe she hadn't heard that right. Maybe it was new slang. Or some kind of gear she knew nothing about. She didn't want to sound stupid, so she just nodded.

"How about you?" Corey asked.

Corey was nice. And brave, to be talking to her where anyone could overhear them, where the grease of her unpopularity might rub off on him. Maybe he was behind that mysterious Christmas present.

"I got something really good from my sister—" Rigel began, and then was interrupted by the noise Hayden and her friends made clattering in.

"Guess who I saw last night at the drugstore," Hayden announced to the room, throwing down her messenger bag. "Corey Green. And he was in the feminine products section!"

So Corey was the one who was getting it this morning.

"What feminine products were you buying, Corey?" Davis asked.

Corey gave a sigh, one so quiet that Rigel was pretty sure no one else heard it. Then he squared his shoulders. "I was there with my mom. I didn't ask her what she was getting. Sorry. What feminine product do you want me to ask her about, Davis?"

Davis turned bright red.

"All right, class, settle down," Mrs. Green said, trying to make herself heard over the usual buzz of chatter. "School Career Day is next week. Class. Class!" Mrs. Green glared around the room until everyone got quiet. "School Career Day is next week. Please ask your parents whether they would be interested in doing a presentation about their career."

"Rigel's mom can come in," Hayden said. "She can tell us all about being a cleaning lady."

Rigel went cold all over. Icy, like she'd never be warm again. How had Hayden known that?

There was only one person who could have told her.

Rigel couldn't see Julie's face, but for some reason she pictured a satisfied smile there.

"Hayden—" Then Mrs. Green fell silent, like she couldn't think of anything else to say.

"What?" Hayden shrugged. "That's what she does."

A low murmur of snickering.

"She makes good money." Rigel forced it out past the lump in her throat. "So what if she cleans houses?"

"Yeah. So what if she cleans houses?" someone said.

The snickers died instantly, like someone had hit a switch to turn them off.

Hayden turned slowly in her seat.

Marion's face was calm and relaxed, but one foot tapped dangerously against the scuffed floor. She said, "My mom cleaned houses. When she came up here from the DR. Then she went to law school. What exactly is your problem with it, Hayden?"

Hayden's mouth opened slightly. Then she put on the look of mild surprise she used on the rare occasions a teacher got mad at her. "Nothing." She said it like she had no idea why Marion was even asking.

Mrs. Green said, "Thank you, Marion. You put that exactly the way I would have wanted to."

"What's the DR?" Rigel asked.

She had no idea why, of all the things she could have said, she chose that.

"The Dominican Republic." Marion was still studying Hayden, who now was searching her messenger bag like there was something important she needed to find right away.

"But your last name is Carling," Rigel said.

"My dad's family is Swedish. My parents met in law school."

Mrs. Green sent around the sign-up sheet for career presentations.

Rigel didn't put down Lila's name.

What would Lila talk about in front of a class anyway? Show everyone her yellow gloves and cleaning buckets? Talk about how much easier it was to keep a house clean when there was running hot water?

Even imagining it made Rigel squirm. But not putting down Lila's name made her feel almost as bad. She couldn't win.

౼౼౼ HHT ౼౼౼

At least it was snowing at lunchtime. Snow in Connecticut slowed everything down and made everything quieter. Cars rolled gently instead of tearing along, pavement disappeared under pillowy white coats, even the train whistle was softer. The falling snow killed its noisy blare.

Plus, when there was more than a few puny inches of the stuff, they usually canceled school.

Connecticut was best in the snow.

Rigel sat on the back stoop, wearing a sweater and her old muskrat-fur hat. Not because she needed the hat to stay warm, but because it still smelled like home. Watching Blueberry peck away at a handful of dog chow, she stretched out her legs and tried to relax.

She can tell us all about being a cleaning lady.

In Fort McPhee, two kids who hated each other like Rigel and Hayden did would fight. It was that simple. They would fight, and afterward things would settle down for a while.

Even better than Fort McPhee would be the cabin, where Rigel wouldn't have to deal with the Haydens of the world at all.

Rigel pulled the dog tag out from under her sweater.

It was warm in her hand, and the silver that had been perfectly shiny last summer was buffed and worn now.

It was her amulet. It was going to take her away from the crowded streets and honking horns of Baldwin. Away from Hayden Foyle and Mrs. Green. Away from pointless homework, banging radiators, tasteless chicken nuggets . . . The dog tag meant that soon Rigel Harman would be back where she belonged.

Although Rigel did have a tiny worry about going back. Actually, it was a worry that wasn't so tiny anymore. It swelled day by day, like a tick she couldn't reach to pull off.

She worried that the Bush might not be *quite* as perfect as she remembered, now that she was softened up by life Outside.

In the Bush, there would be no library or swimming pool that she could walk to, no little shops to explore.

No Grandma. No teachers like Mr. Hernandez or Mr. Trayvick or Mrs. Flores, who was finally managing to teach Rigel some Spanish. No Corey being friendly, or any other kid nearby. Even her sisters would still be in Connecticut. Bear was bringing Rigel back. He hadn't said anything about Willow and Izzy.

That idea was so weird she shoved it to the back of her mind and left it there.

And what about Blueberry?

Somehow Rigel had taken responsibility for the crow. Who would do that after she was gone?

Why couldn't anything be *simple* anymore?

Rigel squeezed her half-eaten apple, then drew back her arm and threw it as hard as she could. It burst against a tree trunk with a messy slap. Blueberry gave a startled squawk and took off into its favorite tree.

Oh no!

You couldn't do things like that around a corvid very many times before it decided you were dangerous and made up its mind to stay away from you.

"Sorry," Rigel said. "I'm sorry, Bluebs."

She whistled. Blueberry rattled cautiously. Finally, Rigel took out the slice of Spam from her sandwich, held it up so Blueberry could see it, and laid it out on the grass under the maple. That finally got Blueberry back down. Blueberry loved Spam.

Chapter 14

Countdown day 201. An ordinary number, an ordinary January, an ordinary Wednesday.

At least the possum was something new.

Rigel had never seen a possum before, although she had heard about them.

It was too bad it was dead.

She squatted on the sidewalk to take a better look.

The possum lay under a ginkgo tree in someone's yard. It had been hit by a car, split open, and then catapulted over the curb. The possum's eyes were still open, its mouth showed sharp yellowy teeth. Life had ended in a second.

That was good, Rigel knew. That it had been quick.

And the possum's remains would be a nice change

of pace for Blueberry. Crows liked carrion, the same way ravens did.

She unzipped her backpack and pulled her gym clothes out of their plastic bag. She picked the possum up neatly by the tail, stowed it in the bag, put the bag in her backpack, and zipped it shut again.

She was going to have to hurry now. She liked to be safe in her seat in homeroom before the buses pulled in and Hayden and her friends spilled out.

But when she pulled open the heavy front door, Hayden was already brushing her hair by the bulletin board, while Marion held her messenger bag and Celeste stood watching.

She made Rigel think of those meerkats they'd seen in a film in science class. The meerkats always had lookouts scanning the area for anything out of place, threatening, or unusual.

Celeste said something to Hayden and Marion, and the three of them turned in Rigel's direction.

Rigel pressed the dog tag against her chest.

She emptied her backpack into her locker—lunch box, gym clothes rolled up, the plastic bag of possum—

Rigel considered the bag again. She hefted it, the way Blueberry lifted a wrapper to figure out whether it was empty or full. And then Rigel had an idea.

A big grin curved her face before she could stifle it.

She hung the plastic bag of possum off the hook in the center of her locker, where it would be the easiest thing to grab, and then shoved the door closed without locking it. She tried to act like she was in a big hurry and just forgot.

The locker door swung back open as she turned away.

Sylvie came up beside her. "Hey, Rigel, you left your locker open."

"Did I?"

Sylvie's forehead wrinkled. "Don't you want to lock it?"

"In a minute," Rigel said.

But she didn't have to wait that long.

A scream split the air behind her.

In front of Rigel's locker, Hayden was jumping up and down, flapping her hands. A screech came out of her like a train whistle. Marion and Celeste stood behind her, bodies tensed like they were ready to run. All of them were staring at the plastic bag on the hall floor—a plastic bag with a possum's naked pink tail sticking out.

Hayden looked so panicked that Rigel almost felt bad for her. Even though she had totally deserved it.

Kids were gathering around.

"Where did that come from?"

"It was in Rigel Harman's locker!"

"Rigel!" Mrs. Kirk snapped. She was the principal. "Come here."

"—oh my God, oh my God!" Hayden was wailing.

"Honey, calm down, it can't hurt you. Celeste, Marion, please take Hayden down to the nurse's office. She's got enough Purell down there to wash an elephant. Then the three of you can wait for me in the main office. Rigel Harman. What was this animal doing in your locker?"

Mrs. Kirk was nice, but that didn't mean she was a push-over. Everything about her, from her neat short Afro to her low-heeled ankle boots, was straightforward and no-nonsense. Rigel's devised excuse, that someone must have left the bag in her locker, suddenly felt pretty flimsy.

"Um, Mrs. Kirk?" someone said. "Excuse me, but I think Rigel was bringing that in for Mr. Hernandez."

It was Corey Green.

"Why would Mr. Hernandez want a dead possum?" Mrs. Kirk asked.

"He didn't ask for a possum specifically," Corey said, "but he asked us to be on the lookout for dead animals that he can add to his bone collection."

It was genius.

Because it was true.

Mr. Hernandez had an assortment of animal skulls and bones laid out on the wide windowsills at one end of his class-room. He had said something about always being on the look-out for more specimens.

Rigel put on the most innocent expression she could manage. "I was going to take it to Mr. Hernandez before class started, but I was running late."

Corey gave her a quick nod, then put on his own inno-cent face as Mrs. Kirk looked back his way.

She rubbed her forehead. "I need another cup of coffee

before I can even begin to deal with all this. You two, please take the possum down to Mr. Hernandez's classroom and leave it there with him. Then, Rigel, you stop by the office before you go to class. I want a chat with you and the other girls before I call your parents. And, Rigel?"

She froze under the scrutiny of Mrs. Kirk's sharp dark brown eyes.

Mrs. Kirk sighed. "I can't believe I even have to say this, but no more dead animals in your locker."

HHT

Mr. Hernandez was surprised by their gift, but also pleased. "This will be a great specimen." He stowed away the possum in the science lab freezer. "Nice and fresh. Extra credit for you both. You know, I'd love a skunk if you ever see one. But leave it outside next time. There's a storage shed by the teachers' parking lot."

They headed back down the hall. Corey going to home-room, Rigel to Mrs. Kirk's office.

"You really saved my butt. I owe you one," Rigel told Corey.

"I just want to know something. What was that possum doing in your locker? Did Davis or Jake put it there?"

"It was mine," Rigel confessed. "I found it this morning by the side of the road."

Corey took her by the arm and dragged her into the stair-well, where no one would be likely to see them.

"Seriously? Why did you put a dead possum in your locker?"

Rigel hesitated. Willow knew about Blueberry. Lila knew about Blueberry. Too many people knew about the crow already. But she owed Corey.

"There's this crow that hangs around out back. By the dumpster and the teachers' parking lot. The possum was for the crow. They eat stuff like that. I've been giving it dog food and hard-boiled eggs and stuff, and I thought the possum might be a nice change."

"Huh." Corey sounded curious, not disgusted. "I've never heard of anybody feeding a crow. Don't they usually do a really good job of feeding themselves?"

"Yeah, but this crow wasn't flying very well for a while. It had a bum wing, and I just got into the habit of helping it out."

Corey peered up the stairwell, making sure no teacher or aide was coming down. The coast was clear, so he took out his iPhone to show Rigel something.

It turned out to be a selfie of Corey sitting on a desk chair holding a big black millipede. Not a regular-sized millipede that was an inch or two long, the kind Rigel saw sometimes in the bathroom. This millipede was as long as Corey's forearm, and its many little black legs, like hooks, clung to the sleeve of his flannel shirt.

"That's my pet African millipede, Millie. 'Millie' is kind of a goofy name," he added, sounding embarrassed, "but I was only eight when I got her. I started out with hissing cockroaches. They're kind of the gateway invertebrate pet."

Rigel was used to all kinds of wild animals, but there weren't many big insects in Alaska. Certainly no foot-long millipedes that reared up on their hind legs, staring into a camera like they were used to doing selfies. She swallowed hard. "Excellent," she said as brightly as she could.

Corey grinned, putting his phone away. "Well, at least you didn't scream and throw the phone, like my cousin Leilani did at Christmas. You've got your pet, I've got mine."

"Blueberry isn't my pet."

"You feed it."

"Just because it was eating crap out of the dumpster."

"And you named it."

"Just because my sister made me."

"Um, okay. You feed it and you named it, but it's not your pet. Fine. You know, you should come to Nature Club sometime. Mr. Hernandez is our advisor. He's okay, he really listens to what we want to do. I brought Millie in once for show-and-tell. We do field trips, we cleaned up the creek—"

"Nature?" Rigel scoffed. "Please. There's no nature here."

"Wow. I've met food snobs, and music snobs, but I've never met a nature snob before."

"But it's true. There's just houses and cars and people everywhere. And—" She racked her brain. "Little pet dogs in sweaters."

That made Corey laugh hard. They were lucky they were in the stairwell, or a teacher would have heard for sure. "Okay, we don't have wolverines and moose and grizzly bears. But, duh, we've got nature here—because we're part of nature, right?"

Rigel opened her mouth, then shut it again so she could think over what Corey had said.

"I mean," Corey went on, "we're not something else. Something outside of it. We're part of it, whether we know that or not."

Rigel squirmed, but she knew Corey was right. "Yeah, I know. I get it. It's just—" She looked around the windowless staircase with its echoey linoleum and flickering fluorescent light.

Corey waited.

"I miss Alaska," she finished. Her eyes prickled and she took a deep breath of the funny-smelling, steam-heated air. "Maybe there is nature here, but there's nothing wild here."

Corey tilted his head sympathetically. "Hey, you know something? My mom grew up in this little tiny town on the Big Island, in Hawaii. And living here gets to her sometimes too. She says everything's always too crowded, and she can never see enough of the sky."

"And at night sometimes the sky is all orange," Rigel agreed. "What's that about?"

"She hates that too. It happens on cloudy nights because of the light pollution."

So that was why.

Corey opened the stairwell door and waited until Rigel realized he was holding it for her.

"Thanks," she managed to say.

"Good luck," Corey whispered as she walked toward the principal's office.

卄卂

The school day should have been over. The buses were gone, the halls were mostly empty. But instead of hanging out back with Blueberry, reading *The Hitchhiker's Guide to the Galaxy*, Rigel was in the principal's office for the second time today, crowded in there with Mrs. Kirk, Hayden, Hayden's mom, and Lila. The little room smelled of coffee and new carpet. Hopefully any lectures would be over fast, because Blueberry was used to having dinner right after school.

"The experience was extremely traumatic for Hayden! She's never had any exposure to a dead animal, ever!" Hayden's mom had the kind of hair that looked windswept, but wouldn't have moved if a hurricane came through. It was dark close to her head and blond at the ends. Frosted, Willow called hair like that. It was a perfect description, because Mrs. Foyle's hair looked like a bundle of leaves left out on the first hard freeze of the year.

Hayden stared past her mom out Mrs. Kirk's window.

"It was very unfortunate," Mrs. Kirk said. "Rigel didn't exercise good judgment. But Mr. Hernandez confirms her story. He made that request at the beginning of the year and Rigel was fulfilling a school assignment. Obviously, it was inappropriate for her to have a dead animal in her locker, and I've made sure she understands that now."

"I have a question." Lila sat in her relaxed way, with one elbow on the back of her chair, but her gaze was fixed on Hayden's mom. Lila shifted, and Rigel caught a whiff of Pine-Sol. "What was Hayden doing in my daughter's locker?"

"I wondered that as well," Mrs. Kirk said.

Hayden put her hands over her face.

What a faker! Rigel would have rolled her eyes, except for the fact that Mrs. Kirk was probably watching her like a hawk.

Hayden's mom patted her daughter's back.

Hayden said, "It was so upsetting I can't even remember."

"That's interesting, because the other girls involved can't remember either." Mrs. Kirk took a sip of coffee.

Hayden's mom said, "Well, it was *traumatic*. I'm not surprised they can't remember!"

"Hayden's locker is all the way down at the other end of the sixth-grade lockers. As are the other girls'. And we're not in the first week of school anymore. It's hard for me to figure out how they could have mistaken Rigel's locker for one of theirs." Mrs. Kirk looked from Hayden to Rigel. "But it doesn't really matter. I'm comfortable with the resolution we've reached on this incident. Unless you want me to pursue it further."

Mrs. Kirk drew the School Handbook toward herself and riffled its pages in a thoughtful way.

Hayden's mom cleared her throat. "As long as Rigel has learned her lesson, I don't think there's any need to do that."

Lila said, "Hopefully Hayden learned one too."

"I'd like you girls to apologize to each other," Mrs. Kirk said. "Rigel, wild animals do not belong in the school building. Hayden, you need to stay out of other people's lockers."

It was almost worth the pain of staying after school to hear Hayden Foyle say "I'm sorry."

HHT

"She's never had any exposure to a dead animal. Good grief." Lila snorted and reached for a paper towel. "Unless she's a lifelong vegetarian, that's not true."

Rigel said, "She's no vegetarian. She eats chicken nuggets all the time."

Every kid in Connecticut ate chicken nuggets. Even Izzy liked them now.

Lila pulled another paper towel loose. She'd said she needed the bathroom, but Rigel suspected they were really giving Hayden and her mom time to leave. "Was that possum for Mr. Hernandez? Or were you taking Blueberry some nice fresh dead meat?"

Lila was settled so comfortably into her new life that sometimes Rigel forgot that her mom had been a bush rat herself.

"I thought it might like a change from all that dog food." Rigel shifted from foot to foot.

Lila bunched up the paper towels and threw them in the trash. "I want to see this crow of yours."

They went around behind the school and sat down on the back stoop. They had barely settled themselves when Blueberry appeared. It flew down out of the maple, eyed Lila, then came forward hesitantly, rattling in its throat.

"Hello," Rigel said.

Kr-rrr.

"Fine, go ahead and be greedy." Rigel took a baggie of dog food out of her jacket pocket and tossed a handful onto the snow. "Enjoy."

Blueberry picked up a dog food nugget, hopped to a pool of snow water, and left the nugget there. The crow did the same with the rest of the pieces before it went back to the first nugget, which was now nice and soft.

"It doesn't seem very afraid of us," Lila said.

Rigel knew this was not a compliment. Wild animals that got too comfortable around human beings came to bad ends.

When they studied biology back in Alaska, Rigel had written a report on a Yellowstone Park wolf named O-Six. O-Six was one of the most successful alpha females anyone in Yellowstone had ever seen: smart, fearless, and quick. People loved to observe her hunting, leading her pack, and raising her cubs. But over time, O-Six got used to being observed, to the constant presence of humans. She must have decided they were harmless. Because the hunter who eventually shot her outside park boundaries said she didn't even try to run away.

She just stood there, watching him, as he trained his gun sight and carefully squeezed the trigger.

Rigel stirred uneasily on the concrete step.

You shouldn't make a wild animal into a pet.

Lila said, "And you never see any other crows around?"

"Maybe a few passing through. But that's it."

"Maybe Blueberry couldn't fly well enough to keep up with them last fall. But it looks like it's flying fine now."

Full of dog food, Blueberry hopped toward Rigel. It stopped to consider Lila one last time.

Lila sat perfectly still, the way she had taught them to do.

Blueberry boldly hopped forward again, onto Rigel's knee. It ruffled up its feathers and waited for a good head scratch. *Kr-rrr*, Blueberry murmured as Rigel scratched the area right around its eyes. That was the crow's favorite spot.

Blueberry's eyes had changed from dark gray to deep black. The crow was growing up.

Rigel leaned her head down, so her forehead touched Blueberry's forehead. The crow liked that too. *Kr-rrrr. Mmmmmm.*

Then Rigel stuck out a finger and Blueberry seized it in its bill and held it there for a few seconds. Blueberry hopped back down and waited until Rigel took a Ping-Pong ball from her jacket pocket.

She held it up so Blueberry could see it, then skittered it over the ground. *Pop-pop* it went along the asphalt. Blueberry hopped after it, biffing it with its bill. The ball went under a parked car. Blueberry disappeared in pursuit.

Lila's eyes were wide, the way Izzy's got when she was surprised. "How much time are you *spending* with this bird?"

"Not that much."

(Almost every day before school, most lunch hours, every day after school, and a quick walk over on the weekends to make sure Blueberry was okay.)

Pop-pop-pop, the ball rolled back toward Rigel across the asphalt. Blueberry waited with its head cocked. This time, Lila reached for the ball and threw it. Blueberry hopped away again.

Lila said, "I keep meaning to ask what ever happened to Julie. You two used to hang out last fall, but I haven't heard anything about her in a while."

"She got busy, I guess."

Lila stayed quiet, watching Blueberry.

Rigel swallowed. "And she wanted— I think she wanted to be friends with different people. More popular people."

"That's too bad. My best friend dumped me like that in seventh grade. It really hurt."

Lila was pretty and funny and smart, the way Willow was. If Lila wasn't popular in middle school, Rigel didn't stand a chance.

Pop-pop-pop, back came the ball toward Rigel.

"But you know what?" Lila smiled as Blueberry let out an excited squawk. "After Elissa Stern dumped me, I started going on Outing Club hikes, and some of those people are still my friends. There's almost always a club or group that's friendly if you don't give up."

These Connecticut people! They were obsessed with clubs. A bush rat like Rigel didn't need any of that.

Blueberry tapped the ball with its bill, flicking it so it rolled right to Rigel's feet.

"I don't need any more friends." Rigel bounced the ball past Blueberry. "I've got Blueberry."

"Blueberry is a crow. You need to be around human beings, the same way Blueberry should be around other crows."

Rigel braced herself for a speech, but it seemed the lecture was already over. Lila had said everything she wanted to say.

Chapter 15

The next morning, Rigel tapped Corey on the shoulder. "Hey, when does Nature Club meet?"

"Huh?" Corey turned around in his seat. "I thought you could care less about our stupid Nature Club."

"My mom says I ought to join something."

That hadn't been the most tactful remark. Luckily, Corey thought it was funny. "We have a lunch meeting today. Bring your lunch to science class, wait for me when it's over, and we can walk up together, okay?"

HH

"Did you get into much trouble about the possum?" Corey asked as they climbed the stairs later.

"Not really. Lila could tell the kind of person Hayden is. And she knows about Blueberry too, so she knew why I would have a possum in my locker."

"I still can't believe you call your mom by her first name. I'm pretty sure my mom would kill me if I tried that."

In Mr. Trayvick's classroom, Sam and Sylvie were sitting at the battered Formica table under the window, their lunch boxes already open. They looked surprised to see Rigel, but Sam dragged his chair sideways so she had space to sit down.

Corey sat next to Sylvie and unzipped his backpack. "Rigel, I guess I should tell you this is an *unofficial* meeting."

"Meeting?" Sylvie didn't sound nearly as shy here as she did in class.

"What are you talking about?" Sam asked.

"You rat," Rigel said to Corey. She couldn't help but laugh. "This is no Nature Club meeting."

"Nature Club? That's every first and third Thursday after school." Corey bit into his sandwich. "This is actually the LHL Club. You know, Losers Having Lunch."

Sam forked some ziti into his mouth. "Bro, I've talked to you about this before. We don't call *ourselves* 'losers.'"

"We're just socially challenged," Sylvie said. Then she shrugged and added, "B-b-b-but we don't really care."

Rigel decided right then that she really liked Sylvie.

"I didn't think we could eat in the classrooms." Rigel punched a straw into her juice box. "How did you manage it?"

Corey bit into an apple and talked through the mouthful. "First we just snuck up here, and then Mr. Trayvick came back one day for something he forgot and caught us. He said it was okay as long as we carried out all of our garbage and wiped down the table afterward."

"And he meant it," Sam added. "There's a bottle of Mr. Clean and a roll of paper towels in the cupboard."

Corey said, "We got tired of the cafeteria, and Princess's reign of terror."

Sylvie tossed an imaginary headful of hair, the same way Hayden did, and said, in a perfect imitation, "'Whatever!'"

That made Rigel laugh. "'Shut up,'" she said back, in her best Hayden voice.

Sam took a box of dominoes out of his backpack. Then a paper plate. Finally a ziplock bag of cookies that he arranged on the plate. "I'm the official club baker. These are tahini cookies. Try one, they're not bad."

"That's what Sam always says," Corey said, grabbing one. "Everything he makes is good."

"I hope you know how to p-p-play dominoes." Sylvie started mixing up the tiles.

"I think everyone in the Bush knows how to play dominoes," Rigel said, helping Sylvie mix, "along with every card game anyone ever invented, because you've got to do something when it's thirty below. Even my dad doesn't like to go outside on days like those. No one even wants to go to the outhouse."

"An *outhouse?*" Sylvie demanded.

"Well . . . yes." Rigel hoped they wouldn't make fun of her. "I mean, we didn't live close to a big town or anything. They have plumbing there. Even if it does freeze all winter long. Then they're stuck using their outhouses too."

"What town were you closest to?" Corey asked. "My mom wanted to know, and I couldn't tell her."

Rigel told them all about Fort McPhee. Corey and his friends didn't think it was boring to hear about Alaska. No one said "Weird!" No one said "Gross!" No one got upset because the Harmans hunted their meat instead of buying it at the supermarket cleaned and wrapped. Instead, Corey, Sam, and Sylvie asked question after question until it was time to put away the dominoes and find the bottle of Mr. Clean.

卌

As they left Mr. Trayvick's room to go to class, Corey waited for Rigel to catch up to him. "So, you're not annoyed or anything, are you? You know, that there wasn't really a club meeting?"

Rigel nudged him. "You're kidding, right?"

"I would have asked you before now, but no one knows where you go at lunch."

He stopped at a hallway window to look out, then pointed

to a big hawk circling up over the trees. He watched the hawk. Rigel watched him.

"Corey, can I ask you something?"

"Sure." He heaved open the safety door and they went down the stairs.

"If I'm not here next year, would you take care of Blueberry?"

"Why wouldn't you be here next year?"

"Just . . . because. Just for some reason."

"I hate to break it to you, Rigel, but we're only in sixth grade. We've got two more years left. At least we're only sixth graders for one year. That's the bright spot."

"Okay, here's the thing," Rigel said quickly. "I'm going back to Alaska next year."

"Really?"

"That's what my dad said." She hoped that she had confided in the right person. "He's bringing me back then."

"Do you think he meant it?"

Rigel stopped short.

Corey shrugged. "It's just, adults say a lot of things they don't mean."

"Yeah, he meant it. Of course he *meant* it."

"Great. Forget I said anything, then."

A cold silence grew between them, like a giant icicle hanging down from a roof.

Then Corey sighed. "When my parents split up, my dad made this huge stink about how much visitation he was going to need and how he wanted us for a month every summer. Blah blah blah. And then he met his new girlfriend and, you know what? We hardly see him anymore. We didn't see him at Christmas this year. He said he had to do Christmas with his new girlfriend and all her relatives. My sister and I each got a gift card and a 'See you at New Year's' kind of deal. He didn't even call on Christmas Day. Did your dad call you?"

"Um, no," Rigel confessed. "But he was working. When he's on, he's working twelve-hour shifts, so he doesn't have any time. He called the next day, though," she rushed to add.

"Too busy for even five minutes to say 'Merry Christmas'?"

It was like Corey was speaking a truth she knew herself but hadn't found the words to say out loud yet. Even when you were working a twelve-hour shift, it wasn't that hard to find fifteen minutes. It took Bear twenty minutes to have a shower, and he showered every day up at Prudhoe. Might as well, he always said, with all that free hot running water.

"Anyway, I'll be happy to take care of Blueberry next year if you . . . If someone needs to take over."

"Oh." Rigel forced a smile.

"But I wouldn't count on it if I were you."

"Okay, Corey. I get it." Rigel started walking faster.

But he walked faster too, to catch up. "Look, I'm sorry if I was crappy about your dad. Whenever I think about my dad, it makes me mad and then sometimes I say dumb stuff."

The bell rang. Rigel had never been so glad to hear its obnoxious clamor. "We'd better get to class."

||||

They had Language Arts next. While Mrs. Green droned on about literary symbolism and kids whispered and shuffled their feet, Rigel thought about what Corey had said.

Do you think he meant it?

Rigel tried to concentrate on Maya Angelou, but the more she tried to forget, the more Corey's words bounced around in her head.

Adults say a lot of things they don't mean.

Corey didn't know Bear. He hadn't even met Bear.

He should just shut up about things he didn't understand.

Alaska people weren't like Connecticut people. They weren't just all hot air and showing off. Alaskans knew how to hang in there, how to keep a promise even when keeping it was tough. Rigel had kept a promise this whole year. She had kept Bear's secret safe, and look what happened the first time she told anyone about it. She wouldn't make that mistake again.

Rigel wasn't going to miss Corey next year.

She wasn't going to miss anything about this pukey place.

After school and Blueberry time, she walked home as fast as she could, her head down, thinking about how much she wanted to talk to Bear. But Bear was either working and pulling a twelve-hour shift, or not working, in which case he would be out at the cabin, and his cell phone was useless there.

When she got home, she tried his cell anyway, just in case. But Bear didn't answer.

Chapter 16

The last Monday in January, countdown day 182.

That morning, a big utility truck was pulled up in the teachers' parking lot, close to the dumpster. Men in hard hats were unloading chain saws, and Mr. Lincoln, in his quilted custodian's jacket, was talking to one of them. He saw her and waved. Rigel waved back and went into school without even bothering to whistle for Blueberry.

There was no chance the crow would hang around with that kind of commotion going on.

At lunchtime, Rigel, Corey, Sam, and Sylvie stared out from the math room window at the men. They had finished their tree trimming and were now at the top of a utility pole, stringing wire.

"You think Blueberry is okay?" Corey asked.

"I think so," Rigel said. "It's not like they could sneak up on it, making all that noise. It probably just flapped over across the street and it's hanging out in one of those trees waiting for them to finish up and go away."

"I bet it's not too happy," Corey said.

"Yeah," Rigel said, "those guys better watch out for their truck."

Blueberry liked to crap all over things that annoyed it.

They all laughed together.

Sylvie and Sam knew about Blueberry now too. Rigel was pretty sure Corey would tell them anyway, so she had gone ahead and beaten him to it.

Rigel and Corey were still friends, even after what he had said about Bear. The way Rigel figured it, he had apologized for what he'd said. And he didn't know Bear the way she did.

Corey, Sam, and Sylvie were okay, for kids from Outside. Actually, they were better than okay. She liked them.

She liked eating in the math room. She made up her lunchtime absences to Blueberry after school, staying extra long and playing game after game of fetch.

Blueberry . . . her lunchtime friends . . . Mr. Trayvick and all his cool math tricks . . . Not everything about Connecticut was so awful. Rigel would have told anyone that now, even Bear.

Rigel said, "Come on, let's eat. I'll check on Blueberry after school."

卌

But after school the men were still working. There was no point hanging out waiting for Blueberry to appear. Even Blueberry wasn't tame enough to hang around a bunch of strangers with noisy power tools.

It was weird to walk home without seeing Blueberry, though.

Rigel knew her friend was okay, but she couldn't help but worry.

She decided to write Bear a good thick letter. It had been too long since she had done that. She'd write him such a good letter that this time he would have to write her back.

卌

The next morning, Rigel got to school extra early. The workmen and their noisy mess were all gone. She stood on the back stoop whistling softly.

Usually Blueberry appeared right away.

Not today.

She checked the dumpster in case someone had fastened the lid tightly and trapped Blueberry inside. But the lid was ajar as usual.

Rigel walked around whistling. She didn't hear any cawing.

No glossy crow flapped down for its breakfast.

For a moment, she thought she heard a caw coming from somewhere, but when she whistled again there was silence. She must have imagined it.

HHT

"How was Blueberry this morning?" Corey asked in homeroom.

Rigel shook her head.

"Blueberry's not out back?"

"No sign of it."

Rigel willed herself to stay calm. Just because Blueberry wasn't out back didn't mean something had happened to it. Maybe it had decided the schoolyard wasn't a good home after all, with all those roaring noises and strange men.

Maybe it had found someone's backyard feeding station covered with peanuts and decided that was a better place to stay.

Maybe it had found a roost full of other birds, even that roost close to Grandma's house.

Just because a bird disappeared didn't mean it was dead.

"What's going on?" Sylvie asked. She and Sam gathered around Rigel's desk.

"Blueberry wasn't out back this morning," Rigel told them.

"You think everything's okay?" Sylvie asked.

Rigel ignored the heaviness in her chest and tried to

sound like Lila, cheerful and relaxed. "There's no reason to think otherwise."

"What are they talking about?" came a voice from behind them. Celeste had noticed them.

Marion shrugged. "Nerd stuff."

"Rigel didn't get a hundred on the math test," Hayden suggested.

"It doesn't have anything to do with hairstyles, Hayden, so I really doubt you'd b-b-b-be interested!"

Hayden's eyes widened with delight. "Sh-sh-shut up, B-B-B-Brookner."

Rigel put a comforting hand on Sylvie's arm. "I'll check out there again later."

HHT

But Blueberry wasn't outside at lunchtime.

HHT

It wasn't there after school either.

HHT

"Rigel, why aren't you eating?" Grandma asked at dinner. "It's Irish stew, you usually like that."

Countdown day 181. Another day over. Another day closer to Alaska.

Then why wasn't Rigel happy? If Alaska was really the only thing that mattered, then why was she so down?

Izzy said, "You'll feel better if you talk about it." Izzy was the kind of person who talked about everything anyway.

"My crow is gone," Rigel said into her plate of stew.

"We can't hear you, honey," Grandma said.

"My crow is gone." Saying the words louder made them feel weightier and more important. "There were some men at school doing tree trimming and stuff around the parking lot. That was yesterday morning. I haven't seen Blueberry since."

"You checked the dumpster?" Lila asked.

Rigel gave her mother a disgusted look. Did she really have to ask?

"Maybe it decided school wasn't safe anymore," Willow offered.

Lila nodded. "It could have finally found some other crows. It could have just moved on, gone somewhere else. Or—"

Rigel finished the sentence. "Something could have happened to it."

Lila looked sympathetic, but her voice was quietly matter-of-fact. "Blueberry's not very careful around people anymore, and that makes it more likely."

Willow squinted across the table at their mother. "Hey, Lila, this isn't Rigel's fault."

"Yeah, that's mean," Izzy said. "Rigel loves her bird! It can't be dead. That wouldn't be fair."

"I think you're forgetting the lessons we learned living in the Bush," Lila said. "Most animals fight hard to survive. Fairness doesn't come into it."

Izzy might have forgotten those lessons. But Rigel hadn't.

On the counter, Willow's phone started buzzing.

"Willow, make that noise stop, please." Lila was always tired on Tuesday nights. Tuesday was her heaviest day, with two huge houses to clean.

"Sorry! I'm just trying to get it charged." Willow jumped up. She glanced at the phone screen before jabbing a button, and didn't look pleased. "God, what is it now? I saw him two freaking hours ago," she muttered, sitting back down.

All of them knew who "he" was. Christian texted and phoned Willow all day long. Willow had liked it at first. But lately it mostly annoyed her.

Rigel couldn't finish dinner, and she didn't even try dessert.

She was upstairs at her table, staring at a page of Spanish homework, when someone's words came unbidden into her mind.

There's a storage shed by the teachers' parking lot.

Mr. Hernandez had said that the day they'd brought him the possum.

A storage shed that the men could have opened up for some reason.

An open storage shed, and a curious crow.

Rigel jumped up and checked the clock by her bed. It was 9:00.

Too late to leave the house without a barrage of questions from everyone. But not too late to make a phone call.

IHT

When Rigel got to school the next morning, Corey and Sam were waiting for her out front. Sylvie had the dentist that morning, or she would have been there too.

Sam had a carton under his arm. Rigel took it from him and checked it: a nice strong box, nothing flimsy about it. It had SALERNO IMPORTERS spelled out on one side and a faded pink towel in the bottom.

"It came from my dad's bakery," Sam said. "And the towel came from our linen closet. I hope I can put it back before my mom finds out."

"You guys know this might turn out to be nothing, right? It's just a hunch."

"We weren't doing anything this morning," Sam said.

"Besides sleeping," Corey joked.

The shed was tucked up against the school building on the other side of the dumpster from where Rigel and Blueberry usually sat. It was made out of battered corrugated iron and its green paint was flaking. The shed door had tired hinges and sagged in the doorframe, but there was a padlock on it—a padlock so shiny and unscratched it must be brand-new. Rigel gave it a quick tug to make sure it was locked.

It was.

Rigel whistled. She didn't hear anything from inside the shed.

"Mr. Lincoln probably has the key," Corey said. "You want me to go ask him?"

Even an adult as understanding as Mr. Lincoln would ask a lot of questions before opening up the storage shed. Maybe he'd need to ask someone else for the key, or even get permission. The more grown-ups were involved, the longer everything would take.

Rigel yanked the padlock again. Not budging.

She walked over to a garden bed edged with brick. One brick sat a little unevenly, heaved out of the ground by frost. She kicked it loose and picked it up.

"Whoa," Sam said.

Corey said, "Do you think that's a good idea—"

Bam.

Rigel smashed the brick again onto the padlock. *Bam! BAM!*

It wasn't the padlock that gave way, it was the cheap latch. The screws sprang out of the doorframe and the latch dangled free. Rigel dropped the brick and heaved open the door.

The inside of the shed was very dark. She could make out stuff like wheelbarrows and rakes jammed inside.

She whistled again. Was that a rustle in return?

"Did you hear that?" Sam said from behind her.

"I can't see *anything*." Rigel slapped the wall in frustration.

"Hold on. I've got a flashlight in my phone." Corey's phone beamed out a stream of light.

Rigel heaved aside a few sheets of plywood. Wheeled a grass-seeder away from the wall.

Blueberry squatted in one corner behind a leaf blower that smelled like gasoline, in its own spattered mess. It didn't move when Rigel approached it, not even to lift its head. Rigel crouched down and used one finger to stroke its feathers.

"Blueberry," she whispered.

Blueberry mewed, so softly Rigel could barely hear it.

"What's wrong with it?" Sam whispered.

"It's been locked in here for two days. No food or water. It's weak," Rigel told him.

"What are we going to do?" Corey asked.

"Let me *think*," Rigel said.

She couldn't just leave Blueberry here.

She couldn't just leave Blueberry outside either.

A sick bird didn't crawl into a warm safe bed and lie there drinking soup. A sick bird was prey for anything that came along.

One of Bear's old sayings came into her head: *A sick bird is a dead bird.*

She could take Blueberry home, but she didn't know how to care for it. Lila would be out cleaning houses, and Grandma would be at her new part-time bookstore job.

The crow needed help now.

"We should get Mr. Hernandez," Corey suggested.

But Mr. Hernandez would be busy getting ready for the school day. He might ask them to wait, or to come back later.

"We need to *take* Blueberry to Mr. Hernandez," Rigel said.

Mr. Hernandez would drop everything to deal with a live bird. He'd have to.

"Are you sure that's a good idea?"

She froze Sam with a quick look. "Do you have a better one?"

"No . . ."

"Then hand me the towel."

Moving slowly, she lowered the towel over Blueberry and, for the first time ever, picked the crow up. It was bigger than she'd expected, but lighter too. Blueberry stirred and let out a squawk. "It's going to be okay, Bluebs," she told it, and put it in the box.

She opened her backpack and took out the baggies she'd brought from home. A baggie of blueberries and cheese cubes, and another baggie with a wad of soaked paper towels. She arranged them inside the box and then shut the carton flaps.

In front of school the buses were arriving. The hall was already crowded. Why couldn't everyone just go to class instead of standing around admiring each other's outfits and YouTube videos?

Blueberry stirred inside the carton.

"Ouch!" someone said. It was Celeste Schenk. Stationed

by the bulletin board as usual. She gave an annoyed huff. "Mrs. Green, Rigel's bashing into everyone with her stupid box!"

Any other teacher would have given an eye roll and let Rigel pass without another word, but not Mrs. Green. She came across the hall.

Rigel felt a sudden jolt from the carton.

"Where are you off to, Rigel?" Mrs. Green didn't sound unfriendly. That was encouraging.

"I just need to take something to Mr. Hernandez," Rigel explained.

Blueberry shuffled again.

Mrs. Green's gaze fell on the box.

The crow scrabbled inside it and pecked the lid.

Mrs. Green's eyes narrowed, the same way Hayden's did when she was annoyed. "Rigel Harman, what do you have in there?" And then, before Rigel could answer, she reached out and tugged up the flaps to check inside.

Blueberry bolted out into the hall.

"Blueberry!"

Rigel hadn't thought the crow had that much strength left. But fueled by fear, it seemed Blueberry had one last fresh reserve. It flapped to the top of the lockers and stood there, beating its wings and cawing an alarm.

Caw-caw-caw! Caw-caw-caw!

Looking fiercely at Rigel.

As far as Blueberry was concerned, Rigel was responsible for putting it in danger.

Worst of all, Blueberry was right.

Kids were screaming and ducking, covering their heads with folders and backpacks and purses. Mrs. Green clamped her arms over her head. Celeste was practically on the floor and even Sam was hunkered down.

Now there was no point in slowly approaching Blueberry or asking everyone around her to calm down. Rigel snatched up the towel and marched across the hall. Blueberry crouched, flapped its wings threateningly, and raised its tail in the familiar way.

Oh *no*.

Bird crap squirted out. Rigel wouldn't have thought Blueberry had any left after that mess in the shed, but it was on the lockers and the wall and on one unlucky girl Rigel didn't even know. (But she was going to have to change her shirt now.) Lightened and ready for action, Blueberry spread its wings and took off again, looking for a high, safe spot.

Toward Mr. Lincoln, who stood there with his usual wash bucket and mop.

Mr. Lincoln's eyes widened with fear. He lifted the mop.

"Mr. Lincoln! *No!*" Rigel shouted. "*STOP!*"

But it was too late. He swung the mop and caught Blueberry across the chest. The crow flew into the wall with a *thump* and then onto the checkered linoleum in a sprawl of blue-black feathers.

Rigel let out a scream that finally made everything freeze.

~~||||~~ |

Sam gently touched Rigel's hand. He sat next to her in the main office, where they were waiting to see Mrs. Kirk. His face was blotched pink.

Corey wasn't sitting. He stood with his arms crossed, staring at the wall. He was mad. Probably at Rigel. She couldn't blame him. She had messed everything up.

Rigel should have just left Blueberry in the shed . . .

She should have never started feeding it . . .

She should have never come to Connecticut.

Mr. Hernandez opened the office door and a man in blue jeans and a flannel shirt, with a headful of graying curls, strode in. He carried a dog crate and had a pair of sturdy gloves under one arm. He moved the way Bear did, like he knew exactly where he was going and what needed to be done next.

"Where's the bird?" the man asked without any polite introductions, like his name or even the word "Hello."

"It's in there." Corey pointed to the SALERNO IMPORTERS carton by Rigel's feet.

Blueberry was safe inside it, although the bird had barely stirred when Rigel carefully transferred it back.

The man lifted the carton off the floor and plopped it onto the secretary's desk. She jumped out of her chair and backed away. He put on his gloves and opened the box flaps.

"This is the man from the Wildlife Trust," Mr. Hernandez explained.

The man reached inside for a moment. There were a few rustles and a squawk. He gave a nod and closed the box again. "Okay, the bird seems comfortable in there, so let's just leave it," he said to Mr. Hernandez. "Can you carry the crate for me?" He stuffed the gloves under one armpit and picked up the carton.

Were they just going to take Blueberry away?

Rigel opened her mouth, but she couldn't find the right words.

"Excuse me," Corey said. "Is Blueberry going to be okay?"

"Blueberry? You mean the crow?" The man put the box back down on the desk and scratched his head, over one ear. "Well, it's weak and sick, possibly injured. I hear a janitor hit it with a mop? I'm sure that didn't do it any good. I'll get it checked out at the Trust and then I'll take it home. If it gets through tonight, that's a good sign."

Rigel's heart dropped clean out of her chest, leaving a cold, hollow spot.

"You the ones who found the crow?" the man went on.

"Rigel found it," Sam said.

The man glanced toward Rigel like she was just another dumb kid in a long line of dumb kids. "It didn't occur to you to let an adult know what was going on? Someone who could have dealt with this in a better way?"

"Which adult do you mean?"

Lila stood in the doorway, her yellow cleaning gloves stuffed through the front belt loop of her jeans. Couldn't she have remembered to leave them in the car?

Lila went on. "Do you mean the adult who let the crow out into a hallway, or the adult who hit it with a mop? I'm Rigel's mom, and from what I've heard, my daughter didn't do either of those things. All she did was try to take the bird to someone who could help it."

A silence fell in the crowded office.

"That's true," Mr. Hernandez said at last. "The kids were bringing the crow to me."

"Oh. I didn't know that." The man glanced from Lila to Rigel. "Yeah. Okay. Um, sorry."

"Now, what's your name?" Lila asked.

"Kevin Brecker."

"I'm Lila Harman. Can we exchange phone numbers? If you could call tonight and let us know how Blueberry is doing, that would be great. My daughter is going to be worried sick."

"Absolutely," he rushed to agree.

In that moment, Rigel forgave her mother for the yellow gloves.

Chapter 17

Suspended," Lila said at dinner.

"Rigel can't go back to school?" Izzy's eyes were round.

"I wish." Rigel pushed lima beans around her plate.

"It's a two-day suspension," Lila told Izzy. "Mrs. Kirk let today count as one of the days. Rigel goes back on Friday."

"I'm not sure I understand what Rigel did wrong," Grandma said.

"Created a disturbance and brought an animal into school again. At least it was a live animal this time."

Rigel thought she saw a smile flicker over her mom's face, but she couldn't be sure, it was gone that fast.

"I wouldn't mind a day off from school." Willow poked at

her pork chop. None of them, not even Lila, liked pork. Pork had a slight resemblance to delicious roast lynx, which made its dryness even more disappointing.

"Rigel isn't going to be relaxing, believe me," Lila said. "She's coming along with me on my cleaning jobs tomorrow. I could use the help. A suspension is not a vacation in this house."

Willow slammed her hand down onto the table so hard all the dishes jumped. "That's typical," she said.

She jumped out of her chair, grabbed her plate, and took it to the sink. Then she let water run over it, a new Connecticut trick all the Harman girls used now when they didn't want to finish their food.

Lila was the only one in the kitchen who didn't seem surprised. She ate a bite of lima beans and waited.

Willow went on. "You bring us down here, and stick us in these schools, and wait to see how everything turns out. Well, maybe no one else has noticed, but Rigel is miserable. She hates it here. She hates everything about it! Now she's been suspended—for no good reason, even Grandma said that—and you can't even be bothered to stand up for her. She gets to spend the day scrubbing toilets with you. Wow. That's so caring."

"How do you know—" Grandma began, but Willow rolled on over the interruption like no one had said anything.

"We never fit in at Fort McPhee because we weren't Native. Now we're in Connecticut, and we don't fit in here either. We don't fit in anywhere but a stupid bush cabin in the middle of nowhere. And now we don't even have that, because you and Bear couldn't suck it up and figure out how to get along like two adults."

Izzy put her thumb into her mouth and stared at Willow over her fist.

"Is there anything else you want to say to me, Willow?" Lila asked.

Judging from the way Willow clenched her fists, she had plenty more to say, but she left the kitchen without another word. The sound of her banged bedroom door upstairs filled their house like a thunderclap.

"Oh boy." Grandma sighed.

"I'll go up in a little, once she's calmed down," Lila said.

"I don't hate everything about Connecticut," Rigel said in a small voice that no one else seemed to hear.

IIII

It was Rigel's night to do the dishes. She was filling the sink with suds and hot water when the phone rang.

It might be Kevin. Blueberry news! For once she ran to the phone and snatched the receiver off the hook. "Hello?"

"Is this Rigel?"

She sagged against the wall. "Hi, Corey," she said.

"Did that obnoxious guy call yet about Blueberry?"

"He said he'd call or text Lila if there was any change tonight. Otherwise tomorrow morning."

"'Any change'? What does that mean, Blueberry dying?"

"I . . ." Rigel stared through the window out at Grandma's pitch-dark yard.

"Oh man, I shouldn't have said that. I'm sorry, Rigel. I'm an idiot."

"It's okay. I think that is what he meant." Still, the idea made Rigel feel sick. "Could you let Sam know what's going on?"

"Yes. He'll be wondering. Sylvie too. Could you text me on your mom's phone when you know something?"

"Okay, I will."

"Text me whenever you find something out. It doesn't matter how late it is."

Rigel hung up just in time to rush to the sink and turn off the water before it overflowed and ran onto the counter. She let some of it out and eased in the glasses and silverware. She leaned against the sink, letting them soak for a few minutes.

She smiled. That was weird. She was worried sick about Blueberry, but there was still a smile on her face.

She wasn't sure when or how it had happened, but Corey was a true friend now.

Definitely.

Sam too. And Sylvie.

That meant Rigel had three good friends besides Blueberry.

Three friends was more than she'd ever had, or even imagined having, back in Alaska.

‖‖‖

Rigel sat on the sofa, staring at the TV.

She didn't have school tomorrow. She could stay up a little later.

Maybe Kevin Brecker would call about Blueberry.

She heard someone coming down the basement steps. It was Lila with armfuls of pillows and blankets. She threw them onto the couch and sat down. "I thought you might like some company. We don't have to talk if you don't want."

Lila spread an afghan over her legs.

Rigel scooched closer to her mom and grabbed an end of the afghan for herself.

They hadn't sat this close together in a long time. Maybe since last summer, since Rigel found out about Connecticut.

A movie was on TV. There were lots of men with their shirts unbuttoned and women in slinky dresses. Lots of expensive handguns and fancy cars.

"Is Willow okay?" Rigel asked after a while.

Lila yawned. "She and Christian had another big fight. She hates the way he tries to run her life, but she's scared about what will happen if they break up. She's worried she'll be the loneliest girl in ninth grade. The big secret is that probably everyone she knows is afraid of the exact same thing."

"They are?"

"Yup, as far as I remember."

Rigel thought of Hayden, Celeste, and Marion, standing

by the bulletin board every day, watching everything that went by.

So worried that something might happen that they didn't know about.

So angry at anyone who wouldn't toe the lines they drew. Even about hairstyles.

That was probably all you had to do to get on their bad side. Be different and be happy that way. Not twist yourself into knots trying to be someone else. No wonder she was on Hayden's list. And no wonder Sam, Sylvie, and Corey were on it too.

On the TV, another car blew up. A woman in a fancy evening gown dove out just before the fireball. Her clothes weren't even messed up.

"I don't know how she can run in those heels." Lila turned down the volume. "Rye Bear? I'm glad you don't hate *everything* about Connecticut."

So someone *had* heard Rigel say that.

"I still hate most things about it," she assured Lila.

HHT

Rigel unwound herself from her blanket and sat up. Lila was curled up asleep at the other end of the couch.

Upstairs, gray light shone in through the kitchen windows. The birds were chattering outside. The black-cat clock said 6:30.

Rigel plugged in the electric teakettle and dropped a tea bag into a mug.

Lila's phone buzzed. She had gotten a text.

Rigel picked up her mom's phone. A message was on the phone screen from KEVIN BRECKER.

Good news, Blueberry made it through the night. All signs positive. Give me a call when you have a chance.

HHT

Rigel whistled all morning while she and Lila scrubbed kitchen counters and changed sheets and mopped floors. They cleaned one big house before lunch. Then Rigel set out their lunches on the kitchen table so they could eat before going on to their next job, and Lila went out to make a call. When she came back, she said, "That was Kevin Brecker. Blueberry's doing well. Fine and feisty, and gobbling down everything Kevin offers it."

"Oh, that's great! When can I visit?" Rigel asked.

"Blueberry is thin and dehydrated. And it has a broken clavicle." Lila touched her own collarbone. "Probably from the mop. That'll take four to six weeks of cage rest to heal. Blueberry should be released this spring. Maybe early April."

Rigel wondered why Lila didn't look happier if it was all such good news. "So, when can I see Blueberry?"

Lila took a deep breath, like someone about to jump into deep water. "Now for some bad news."

Rigel put her sandwich down.

"There are rules about wildlife rehabilitation. One rule is that the people doing the rehab have as little contact with the animals as possible. They don't want them to imprint on human beings. They don't want them to get tame. They want them to stay wild."

That all made sense. "Okay."

"Another rule is no visitors."

That couldn't be right.

"Especially no underage visitors," Lila emphasized.

"But I'll be careful. I'll do whatever Kevin tells me to do."

"He wants to keep Blueberry wild, Rigel. Blueberry's in wildlife rehab, not the zoo. People don't get to just go and visit whenever they feel like it."

In other words, Lila was on Kevin's side. She thought Kevin was right. Of course she did! Adults always stuck up for each other.

"But it's not fair! I'm not some dumb kid."

"Maybe I can get him to send some pictures. I'll try, okay? And one more thing."

"*What?*" Rigel snapped.

"When Blueberry gets released, Kevin will probably do the release over where he lives. That's about twenty miles from here. There are a lot of crows living in those parts, and since Blueberry doesn't have a family group here, Kevin thinks it'll do just as well over there."

That was probably true. But it also meant that Rigel would never see Blueberry again.

No one even cared that the crow had been her friend. No one cared what she thought about any of it.

It was just like last spring when they'd told her about Connecticut.

"Rye Bear, I did warn you that it was not a good idea to make Blueberry into a pet."

Rigel smashed her sandwich into a ball and stuffed it back into the paper bag. "I *hate* you."

Lila's face turned pink, like she'd been slapped. "At least that's a change from you whining about how much you hate being here."

Chapter 18

Rigel and Lila had another house to clean, and they didn't speak one unnecessary word to each other while they vacuumed and scrubbed. When they got home, Lila grabbed the weekly grocery list off the refrigerator. "I've got a bunch of errands to run, but I should be home for dinner. Tell Grandma."

She left for the supermarket without asking Rigel whether she wanted to come along.

It would have been a good day to find a postcard from Bear. But there was nothing.

As usual.

Nothing since their Christmas cards. Not even a post-card, let alone a phone call.

But, peeling her afternoon orange, Rigel had a thought.

Even if Bear was too busy to talk, Kimora wasn't.

Rigel always forgot that Kimora's family had a phone. Rigel's family had only ever had the satellite phone, for emergencies. But in Fort McPhee almost everyone had a regular phone nowadays.

And Kimora would know how Bear was doing. Everyone in the Bush knew one another's business.

"Worse than a church choir," Rigel whispered out loud.

Rigel went into Lila's room, where Lila kept her address book in the top drawer of her desk, and then carried the address book into Grandma's room, where there was a phone on the bedside table. She dialed. The phone rang twice and then got picked up on the other end, all the way across the North American continent, in the village of Fort McPhee, Alaska.

"Hello," Kimora said.

"Hey!" Rigel said. "It's me."

"Rigel?"

"Yeah. I just wondered how you've been doing."

"You're lucky I'm home, genius," Kimora said. "It's twelve o'clock here!"

Rigel smacked her forehead with the palm of her hand. She had forgotten all about the time difference. Connecticut was four hours ahead of Alaska.

"I can't believe you forgot." Kimora laughed.

"Why aren't you in school, then?"

There was a pause. "I'm sick."

"Yeah, right," Rigel said, and Kimora laughed again. School wasn't Kimora's favorite thing.

She asked, "How's Connecticut?"

"All right," Rigel heard herself say. Had those words really come out of her?

"See? I knew you'd get used to it. It can't be that bad. I think you're forgetting what it can be like around here."

"That crow I wrote you about? Blueberry? It got in trouble. It got hurt."

"Serious? Is it dead, then?"

"No, but they took it to a wildlife rehab place. I probably won't . . . I probably won't see it again."

"Aww. That's too bad, Rigel."

Rigel considered how to bring up Bear while Kimora went on talking.

"It sounds like a lot of fun down there to me. It's been boring here this winter. No dances or anything. And you know something *really* weird? The snow's already getting soft. Mom says she's never seen it warm up this quick before. The hunting hasn't been too good. Lucky Uncle Preston got that moose or we'd be eating frozen fried chicken and Spam." Kimora heaved a heavy sigh. "This place is such a dump. Me, I can't wait till I'm eighteen. Fairbanks, here I come."

"Have you seen Bear lately?" Rigel kept her tone casual. "Has he been coming through town now and then?"

"I guess you could say that. Hanging around the store night and day, you know?"

Of course Bear would be passing through regularly, on his way to and from Prudhoe. Still, Rigel couldn't guess why he would be spending hours in the store. The village store had started out as a lean-to attached to the post office. Even now, fancied-up with walls and doors, it wasn't big enough for anyone to spend hours inside.

"Is he in town now?" Rigel asked.

"Yeah, he's always here now. Him and Paulette, you can't pry them apart."

"Paulette?" Rigel said.

"Paulette Thompson. You forget all about her, huh?"

There was a Paulette Thompson who was Wilfred Thompson's niece. She worked at the village store and had a little boy. She'd had him with her high school boyfriend, who'd left Fort McPhee after graduation and never come back, the way it happened sometimes.

"You mean Wilfred's niece?"

"No other Paulette Thompson I know."

This was an idea that was going to take getting used to. Rigel swallowed. "He can't always be in town. He's working at Prudhoe."

"Huh? He hasn't been up at Prudhoe since Christmas."

"What?"

"Yeah, Paulette didn't like him being away that much.

He came back right before Christmas and he's been here ever since."

Rigel sat very still.

"You knew that . . . right?" Kimora wasn't laughing anymore.

"I've got to go," Rigel said, and hung up.

Corey's words from all those weeks ago came into her head loud and clear.

You know, when my parents split up, my dad made this huge stink about how much visitation he was going to need . . .

And then he met his new girlfriend . . .

She dialed Bear's number. It went to voicemail, the way it always did now. And because Bear never deleted any of his old messages, it was always *This mailbox is now full.*

Rigel hung up. She sat staring at the stuff on Grandma's bedside table.

Clock radio.

A vase with daisies in it.

A big blue button lost from someone's coat.

The slim rectangle of Grandma's cell phone.

She'd forgotten it this morning. Grandma forgot her phone a lot.

Rigel picked the phone up and pressed the little round button to make it turn on.

She called Bear's number again.

For no reason. Just because.

Only, this time, Bear answered. "Hello?"

Rigel was so surprised she couldn't talk, not right away.

"Hello? Who is this?"

"It's me," Rigel said.

"Rigel?"

"Yeah."

"Well." Bear sounded taken aback, but then he rallied. "Well—hey! How are you doing, Rye Bear?"

"Was it okay for me to call you?" Rigel asked.

"Well, yeah, sure," her father said. "Where are you calling from, though? This isn't your home number." He chattered straight on without letting her answer. "How are things going for you down there in the plastic paradise?"

Suddenly Rigel was sick of the way Bear always talked about Connecticut.

What made him such an expert? He'd never even been here!

"How's the Slope?" she asked.

There was a long pause.

"Okay, who have you been talking to?" Bear said. "Who's been pouring poison in your ear?"

Now it was Rigel's turn to be silent.

"It was Lila. Boy, I bet she just loved telling you that whole story."

"It was not Lila," Rigel said. "Kimora told me. And I bet it's true about Paulette Thompson too."

"Rigel—" Bear broke off what he was about to say. "Paulette's always liked you girls. She told me that, right off."

"She doesn't even know us."

"Sure, she knows you. She remembers you from when we used to visit Wilfred. Everyone knows each other in Fort McPhee anyway." He tried out a chuckle, maybe to see if she would join in. "Anyway, she really wants to get to know you. She wants to get to know all you girls."

"I guess I'll see her this summer, then."

Bear didn't say anything.

"I'm still coming back, right?"

"Well, we've got some stuff to work out first, but I hope so."

"What kind of stuff?"

"We've got to sell your mother on the idea, we've got to find the money . . . I'm not making those big bucks up on the Slope now. It might take a little longer to get our ducks in a row, that's all I'm saying."

Another silence. This one was broken by a woman's voice speaking up on Bear's end.

Bear said, "I need to get going, kiddo."

"Why? It's not like you're going to be late for work or anything."

"Whoa! You know who you sound like right now? You sound like your mother, and believe me, her nagging is not something I miss."

"Too bad." Rigel hung up.

Chapter 19

The Wizard of Oz was on and Rigel watched that for a few minutes before turning it off. Then she lay on Grandma's sofa, staring at the stack of laundry baskets across the room. Sounds were muffled in the basement. She couldn't even hear cars whooshing by, or the whistles of the New York trains. It was like being underwater.

Outside, groups of laughing kids passed the house on their way home from club meetings or sports practices. Their chatter was so loud it even penetrated her refuge in the basement.

Rigel suddenly sat up. Grandma would be getting home any minute from the bookstore, and Izzy would be with her, fresh from her after-school program.

Rye Bear! Look at the picture I made!

Rigel! Rigel! Watch me, I can do a cartwheel!

Rigel, can you help me cut my apple, pleeeeeeeeease?

Rigel loved her little sister, but she couldn't listen to that. Not right now. Not today.

She scribbled a note saying she was taking a walk and left the house.

She shoved her fists into the pockets of her jacket and stood on Grandma's lawn, wondering where to go.

She could go to the Lee Price Chappell Wilderness and walk along its worn paths with bunches of dog walkers and stroller moms . . .

Walk downtown to the library and see if they had any new books . . .

A blue jay screeched close by. Rigel couldn't see it. Out of habit she walked to the little waste ground bordering the railroad tracks to see if she could spot it, but it was nowhere in sight. Then Rigel started walking north along the railroad tracks. For no reason. Just because.

She passed the crow-roost trees, a few tall oaks under a streetlight. There were no crows in them, because it wasn't nighttime yet, but the trunk and branches were all well streaked with crow whitewash.

She walked through people's backyards along the football-field-wide strip of trees and brush with soggy patches of snow under them.

February, and the snow was already melting!

And they called this winter. Pathetic!

She waited for someone to yell at her, *Get out of my yard!* Or, *What do you think you're doing, kid?* But no one was home or, if anyone was home, no one was looking outside. She trudged along beside the tracks.

She was alone, but also, in the weird ways of Outside, not alone.

Maybe she just needed to talk to Bear again. This time she'd stay calm. She wouldn't lose her temper and she'd laugh at all his jokes. She'd tell him he was right about Connecticut being a plastic paradise and she'd act happy about Paulette. They could come up with a new plan. She could start a new countdown. Even though she was already something like 50 percent through the old one. (She did some quick math; it was actually 49 percent.)

Yeah, right, Willow's voice said in Rigel's head.

Only 49 percent of the way through their countdown, and Bear already had a new girlfriend and had quit Prudhoe. Even worse, Rigel had found out from Kimora. What a fool she must have sounded like! Kimora probably felt sorry for her. She might be saying to someone right now, "You want to know something weird? I was talking to Rigel Harman today and I don't think she knew about Bear and Paulette. I said something about them, and she was surprised, I swear."

That news would go through Fort McPhee like crap through a goose. Pretty soon everyone would know.

When had Bear been planning to tell Rigel? Maybe he hadn't worried about it. Maybe he never even thought about her anymore. Or maybe he had just been waiting for her to find out somehow. Like the time Lila opened her wallet in the Fort McPhee store to buy groceries and there was only half the money inside she'd expected and that was how she had found out that Bear had lent someone money without asking her first. They had had to put back some of the groceries, the Tang and Spam and cake mixes, and Lila had been so mad. Now Rigel could understand why.

She came to a big four-lane road. There was a traffic light there and not many cars anyway, so it was easy to cross.

More backyards. Squirrels flicking their tails and stopping to glare at her. Skinny deer looking up from dining on people's rosebushes and rhododendrons.

Was Rigel going back to Alaska or not?

Well, we've got some stuff to work out first, but I hope so, Bear had said.

Stuff to work out?

I *hope* so?

They'd had a deal! When they made their promise, there was nothing about *I hope so.* There was nothing about *stuff to work out first.*

She'd kept her end of the bargain. She'd done everything Bear had asked her to do. Down to keeping their secret for months, even when it felt like a heavy chain she had to drag along. What kind of deal was it when one person did what they promised and the other person didn't?

It was a deal like the overflow ice back home in Alaska,

the ice that looked so strong and sound until the moment you put your weight on it and went through—*smash*. It was just like that.

Rotten ice, rotten promise.

Another busy road with a traffic light, red this time. She waited for it to change, tapping her fingers on the light pole, and then crossed. On the other side of the road, there was a small parking lot full of cars. And a dark brown wood sign with orange letters and an arrow pointing down the trail.

EAGLE ROCK NATURE SANCTUARY, the sign said.

Nature! That was a joke. No matter what Corey had said. Probably full of yapping little dogs and people walking along looking at their phones. It was bad enough that they stared at them all the time inside. Staring at a phone outside was something Rigel would never understand.

There was another little sign at the edge of the trail, and Rigel walked a few feet into the quiet woods to see what it said. This one had an arrow pointing at a narrow path that led upward.

SCENIC OVERLOOK.

It probably overlooked a highway. Or a parking lot full of cars.

But it might be good for a laugh.

Rigel glanced up at the sun. It was getting low, but she had enough time to get back before it was too late. She followed the path into the woods. It kept climbing, not steeply but steadily. A man passed her with a dog on a leash, and after that there was no one else coming down the path toward her. She kept hiking up until she finally came out into a clearing skirted by birches. This was the Scenic Overlook.

There was nothing in front of Rigel but empty space and the tops of trees. She walked forward, hypnotized by the view.

A woman sat on a bench with a pair of binoculars in her hand. She had a friendly face, with pale blue eyes and short brown hair. The sweatshirt she wore said EAGLE ROCK NATURE SANCTUARY, BIRCH GROVE, CT.

Birch Grove was two towns north of Baldwin.

Rigel had taken a long walk.

She went to the edge of the cliff. Although it wasn't exactly a cliff. It was more like a very steep hill—she could have scrambled down it—but it was rocky, and the rocks and boulders kept the trees and scrub from growing up and blocking the view. Rigel could see out for quite a distance. It must have been miles.

If she'd known about this place, she would have started coming here a long time ago.

Two birds came into sight. At first Rigel could barely make them out. They were like little bits of black cloth skimming through the sky. Swooping, diving, doing loop-de-loops for the fun of it—

Rigel gasped. There was only one type of bird she knew that would fly like that.

"Are those *ravens*?"

"Aren't they fabulous?" The lady on the bench put

her binoculars to her eyes. "It's that nesting pair from the radio tower."

"There aren't any ravens here."

"There weren't. Not for a long time. But they're coming back now. This pair has a nest in the radio signal tower. They've been there for a few years."

In a radio tower?

It did make sense. It was a good place for a raven nest, high up, hard for predators to reach.

"They were raising three fledglings last spring, but a raccoon got up there somehow and ate them all in a single afternoon." The lady took the binoculars away from her eyes, scratched one eyebrow, and raised the binoculars again. "And then it had a long snooze in the nest afterwards. I was so mad."

The lady talked the way Alaskans talked. They gossiped about animals the way they gossiped about human beings.

The ravens spun, dropped, whirled in the air.

"Maybe those ravens are from Alaska," Rigel said.

"Ravens only migrate short distances," the lady said firmly. "No, those are Connecticut ravens."

Anyway, they were ravens, and they had found a way to live here. They lived on a radio tower, instead of at the top of a tree, and they had probably found a dumpster with a plentiful supply of pizza crusts and candy wrappers. They were here, that was the important thing. And look at them play!

They were black whirligigs against the purple-blue sky.

Purple?

In the west, a red glow clung to the sky, fading fast. Other than that glow, the sky was dark. It was late.

The lady got up from the bench and dusted off her butt. She put her binoculars away in their case. She said, "Well, it looks like it's takeout for dinner again."

"Do you have the time?" Rigel asked.

"Just after six."

"Six!"

They usually ate at six. And she had a long walk home ahead of her.

"Do you need to use my phone?" the lady called after Rigel, but she was already skidding down the trail, going as fast as she could.

Was she going to be in trouble. Even if she ran all the way, she was going to be late. When she got to the four-lane road, she decided to walk on its shoulder. That would be faster. She took off her jacket so her pale shirt would show up in the dark, but even so, the cars flying by made her nervous.

There was a loud blat of honking across the road that made her jump, as a car did a U-turn. Then, to Rigel's surprise, the battered little car cut across two lanes of traffic, causing more indignant honking. It jerked over onto the shoulder ahead of her and only then did Rigel recognize it.

It was Uncle Vance's old Civic, and Lila was behind the wheel.

||||

Sitting at the kitchen table in front of her warmed-up dinner, Rigel tried her explanation one more time. "I left a note—"

"'Going for a walk.' That was all it said! Nothing about where you were going! Nothing about when you'd be back! Your mother and I were out of our minds with worry. Driving all over town trying to find you. I was about to call the police. The police!"

"Mom, I gave Rigel the full lecture in the car." Lila was repeating herself too. "I really think—"

Grandma ignored this. "You may be only eleven years old, young lady, but you're old enough to show some consideration for the people who love you!"

Rigel glared. "In Alaska I did stuff like that all the time!" she said. Which wasn't true. Even in Alaska, she told Lila or Bear where she was going, and they knew when she should be back.

"Your grandmother thought you had run away." Lila sounded tired.

"Run away where?" Rigel asked.

"Back to Alaska, of course," Grandma said.

Didn't Grandma know anything about Alaska?

How would Rigel get to Anchorage or Fairbanks? How could she ever afford the plane fare? And even if she could reach Fairbanks somehow, how would she get from the city to their place in the Bush? Did Grandma imagine Rigel could walk home from Fairbanks, maybe on a nice wide sidewalk? Or take an Uber?

Good grief, there wasn't even a road out to their cabin!

And it wasn't like Bear lived there now anyway.

Grandma took off her glasses and rubbed her eyes. "I don't know what to do. I'm out of ideas. It's no secret Rigel isn't happy here. I knew there was going to be an adjustment period, but . . ." She opened her hands, like she was letting go of something. "Lila, maybe we should think about letting Rigel go back."

Lila wrinkled her forehead. "Go back where?"

"Back to Alaska."

Rigel's heart gave a funny jump in her chest.

Lila's face went ghost-white. "That option is not on the table, Mom."

"It might be better than her living here and being miserable. Maybe we should talk about it, that's all I'm saying."

For one moment, Rigel was soaring. She was a raven flying over the cliffs, flying north and west toward the Arctic while suburban Connecticut shrank to broccoli and bits of colored paper far below. But her flight didn't last longer than that second before she jolted back down to earth. She was plain old Rigel Harman again, in a yellow sweatshirt and her sister's old jeans that were still too big for her, sitting in front of a plate of food she didn't want.

"Grandma, don't be silly. I'm not going back."

Grandma and Lila stopped arguing. "Why would you say that, Rigel?" Grandma asked.

"Bear doesn't want me."

220

When Rigel solved a math problem, sometimes she knew exactly how she did it and could explain the steps. Other times, she didn't know how. She just made a jump somewhere. It was hard, almost impossible, to explain how she discovered the right answer.

The stack of postcards up in her room, getting grimy around the edges from being read and reread because Bear hadn't sent a new one in so long—

Always getting Bear's answering machine, except for the one time she called him from a different phone—

Bear's vagueness about when she was coming back and how they would pay for it—

Dominoes toppled, one after another, *click click click*. Once they were all down on the table, their pattern was obvious.

The only question was how she had missed it for so long. But then, she hadn't, not really. Some part of her had known. It had known for a while. Probably since that time Corey had said *Do you think he meant it?*

"He never writes anymore, and he almost never calls . . . not even at Christmas. He's not at Prudhoe the way he said he was going to be, and"—Rigel took a deep breath—"he's got a girlfriend now. I think I'd just mess everything up for him."

Grandma said, "Oh, Rigel."

"Rye, I'm sorry." Lila sat down next to her at the table. "I know how much you want to be there. I know, because I miss it too. But I can't imagine living here without you. We're still a family, you know, even after everything that's happened."

"Are we?"

Lila wasn't Mrs. Green. Lila didn't say anything to make Rigel feel small.

She put her hands on Rigel's shoulders and leaned over so their foreheads touched.

"Yes. We are. I know things have changed, and it's been weird, and you've hated a lot of it. But we're still a family."

Grandma was wiping her face. Lila's eyes were wet. If Rigel started crying too, it was going to be a mess all the way around. She blinked hard and said, "That's good."

She squeezed Lila's hand, and Lila squeezed hers back, hard, like she'd been waiting a long time to do it.

IIII

After dinner, Rigel went outside.

She stepped carefully over the uneven flagstones of the back patio and walked over to the pine tree by the railroad tracks.

She pulled the dog tag from her neck.

She had worn it every day. It was the first thing she put on in the morning and the last thing she took off at night, after the lights were out. She did that so Izzy wouldn't see it and ask a bunch of dumb questions.

But, really, Izzy wasn't dumb.

Rigel was the dumb one.

She wound the silver chain around the dog tag to make a

tidy package and then drew back her arm and threw the package as hard as she could down the tracks. It was heavy enough to fly straight and true. In the dark, she couldn't see where it went, and she didn't hear any noise to mark where it fell.

She stood there until someone's car alarm pierced the night and drove her back inside. Even though it was still early, she went upstairs to bed. She was tired. She felt like sleeping for a really long time.

Chapter 20

The next morning, Rigel found a few photo printouts on the kitchen table.

One showed an angry Blueberry in a wire cage. Blueberry had its eye turned to whoever was behind the camera and its bill was open, ready to give a cruel nip to anyone dumb enough to put a finger inside. In another picture, Blueberry was attacking a plastic rubber duck, some kind of dog toy. That ducky wasn't going to last long. The third photo showed a cage covered with the remains of a torn-up plastic sheet and Blueberry glaring out from under the shredded fringe.

"Is that your crow?" Still in her pajamas, Willow peered

over Rigel's shoulder at the picture. "Did you talk to Kevin? How is Blueberry doing?"

She was looking at Rigel, but Lila was the one who answered. "Kevin said when he came out this morning Blueberry had torn down all the tarps over its cage and shredded them overnight. I think we can assume it's feeling better."

"That's great." Willow glanced from Lila to Rigel. "Isn't that great, Rye?"

Rigel picked up a printout and studied Blueberry in its cage. She could tell from Blueberry's open bill, from its fixed glare, how terrified and angry her friend was. "Yeah. Great."

She noticed Willow and Lila glancing at each other. Lila bit into her toast. Willow helped herself to the oatmeal on the stove. Rigel put her dishes in the sink and stuffed the printouts into her backpack. She left for school without saying anything else to either of them.

HHT

Rigel was barely inside the school doors when an older girl with curly red hair came up to her.

"Your bird pooped on me a few days ago."

That was why the girl looked familiar.

"Oh geez. I'm sorry about that. It was really upset."

The girl nodded. "It's okay. I mean, it was gross, but I

understand. My mom told me it's good luck. I decided to believe her because otherwise it's just too disgusting. Anyway, how's the crow doing?"

"It's still alive." Then Rigel admitted, "Actually, it's doing well."

"That's good news. Oh—by the way, my name's Bella. Got to go, but I'll see you around."

HHT

Rigel was at her locker when Mr. Lincoln appeared beside her.

"I just wanted to say I'm so sorry about that crow friend of yours," he said.

"It's okay."

"It took me by surprise, that's the truth. It was what you call instinct. How's it doing, Rigel, do you know?"

Rigel showed him Lila's pictures.

"Looking lively." Mr. Lincoln took a closer look. "Hmm. I wouldn't want to put a finger in that cage."

HHT

Homeroom was more of the same.

Davis said, "Was that crow yours or something? What happened to it?"

"Why was it even in school?" Marion wanted to know.

"Shouldn't it be dead? Mr. Lincoln hit it really hard. It was there in the hallway and then next thing, *pow*." Jake swung a fist through the air.

"Where is it now?"

"Did you take it home?"

Rigel took out the pictures and almost everyone crowded around to see.

"I can't believe everyone's making this big fuss about one stupid crow," Hayden said from her desk.

No one paid attention. Not even Marion. She was craning over Sylvie's shoulder, trying to get a look at Blueberry destroying the plastic ducky. Sylvie took the printouts from Rigel's hand and laid them out on Mrs. Green's desk to make it easier for everyone to look.

Julie pushed past Davis to pick up a picture and study it.

She looked from the printout to Rigel. And then she smiled. Like nothing had ever happened between the two of them. Like they were just starting a friendship, instead of being two people who had failed at it.

What was *that* all about?

Rigel dropped into her chair and flipped open the library book she had finished last night. She pretended to study a random page like it was the most interesting thing she'd ever seen. When she looked back up, Julie had settled into her desk. It looked like she was busy with some homework. She didn't look Rigel's way again.

᚛᚜ ||||

After science class, Rigel stayed for a few minutes to talk to Mr. Hernandez.

"The man who's doing Blueberry's rehab said I can't visit."

Mr. Hernandez nodded as he cleaned something off the whiteboard. "That sounds hard, even if it's for a good reason."

"Everyone says I shouldn't have made Blueberry into a pet."

"There are always people who see the world in black and white." Mr. Hernandez put down the eraser and turned to face her. "It doesn't sound to me like Blueberry was your pet, not exactly. Let's just say there's a bond between the two of you. You're important to each other."

"Blueberry was my friend."

"Past tense, Rigel? Blueberry's still alive. Maybe you'll see it again someday."

"Even if they do release it, there's no reason for it to come back here. It probably won't. It got hurt here, so it'll stay away."

"It might surprise you."

Rigel shook her head.

Mr. Hernandez leaned back against his desk and crossed his arms. "You know, when I was in middle school, they taught us that birds were stupid. Nothing but instinct, no reasoning ability at all. That's why people say 'birdbrain' when they want to call someone dumb."

"You're kidding!"

"I'm not kidding. That's what the experts believed. Rigel,

we learn new stuff about animals every day. We still don't know all that much about what they're capable of in terms of behavior. About how they think or what they think about. Whether they have emotions, if they're capable of love. I don't know if you'll see Blueberry again. What I'm saying is that maybe you're Blueberry's friend, the same way Blueberry is yours. Just something to think about. Here, let me write you a hall pass. You're going to be late."

�﬩

At lunchtime she headed upstairs, hoping for one of Sam's treats or a good game of dominoes. But when she came out of the stairwell on the second floor, there were unhappy voices coming from Mr. Trayvick's room.

"We've been eating lunch all semester in here." Corey's voice.

"Mr. Trayvick said we could." Sam's voice now.

"You can ask him," Sylvie suggested.

"I can't ask him when he's not here, Sylvie. You three get your lunches and go down to the cafeteria and eat there, like everyone else."

Mrs. Green again! Why couldn't she just sit in the faculty lounge at lunch like the other teachers?

The kids came out of the classroom scowling, followed by Mrs. Green.

"Rigel Harman," she said, not sounding surprised.

She escorted them all the way down to the cafeteria in her usual way. They stood inside the doors, looking around. It smelled like hot dogs and burned tomato sauce.

A table toward the back was empty at one end. They hurried over before someone else could sit there.

Sam, as usual, started taking item after item out of his backpack.

First the domino tiles.

And then a Tupperware container and a plate.

He opened the container and arranged mini cream puffs frosted in chocolate into a neat pyramid. "This is my first try at these," he said, "and they probably won't be very good. I had a lot of trouble tempering the chocolate, for some reason . . ."

It was the kind of stuff Sam always said about his creations. But none of them touched the pastry, or the dominoes. It was weird being in the cafeteria again.

"Are we going to play today?" Sam finally asked.

"I don't know." Sylvie looked uneasy. "Someone will p-p-p-probably make fun of us."

"They'll make fun of us no matter what we do." Rigel said it louder than she meant to.

"Rigel's right. Come on, let's play." Corey dumped the tiles out on the table and started turning them over and mixing them up.

They all helped. You had to mix the tiles up really well. That was one of the secrets to a good game of dominoes.

Corey said, "Hey, Rye. Nature Club, this week. We're having the organizational meeting for next year. You in?"

Rigel flipped over a domino that had gone face-side up. "Okay."

Sam, Sylvie, and Corey stopped mixing.

Sam said, "You're kidding. No, you're serious."

"I didn't think you were ever going to show up," Sylvie said. "What changed your mind?"

That was a long story. Rigel was considering whether to even launch into it when she noticed Hayden, at the front of the cafeteria, get up from her table, laugh at someone's joke, and then throw the remains of her lunch in the trash.

Hayden's head swiveled as she looked around.

Rigel thought Hayden might have noticed them.

Then Celeste and Marion looked in their direction too, and her suspicion became a certainty.

The bulletin board girls walked over to their table.

"Are those dominoes?" Marion said. "My *grandfather* plays those."

"That's fascinating, Marion." Corey kept mixing tiles.

Hayden looked at Sam, who was biting into his cream puff. "Are you really going to eat that?"

Sam put down the cream puff, with his teeth marks in its chocolate glaze, and ducked his head.

"I can't watch," Celeste chimed in. "No wonder he looks like a whale."

Giggles started bubbling up around them.

Then Rigel slammed her hand down onto the table and stood up.

"You don't like watching Sam eat?" she said. "Then stop watching and go away."

It wasn't anything clever, but it was the best she could do.

Hayden's eyes narrowed in her signature way. "Excuse me?" It was always a bad sign when she was this polite. "Who do you think you are? Get over yourself! We'll go when we feel like it."

Rigel groped for the comfort of her dog tag.

But it wasn't there.

No one was taking her away from here.

If anyone performed a rescue, it would have to be Rigel herself.

She stepped forward, so close she caught a whiff of the chicken nuggets on Hayden's breath.

"Move it," Rigel said. It was what Bear would have said. "And you can take your two winged monkeys with you."

Someone laughed. Someone at the next table over. Then the laughter spread toward the front of the cafeteria, where the popular kids sat.

Hayden, Marion, and Celeste looked at one another. Then Hayden pushed her hair over her shoulders.

"Oh, come on," she said. "Whatever. I've got better things to do."

They strolled back toward the big double doors, their heads together, as always.

"Rigel. You can sit down now." Sylvie patted the bench beside her. Rigel sat. "That was amazing, by the way."

"Rigel scared her away forever," Sam said. Rigel gave him a skeptical look. "Okay, maybe not forever." He picked up his cream puff, the one with teeth marks, took a bite, and licked his thumb.

"Maybe we should have asked Hayden whether she wanted one," Corey said, helping himself.

Sylvie shook her head. "There's no sweetening Hayden up."

"She's always so cranky," Rigel said. "She makes me think of a character in this book *The Hitchhiker's Guide to the Galaxy*. Marvin the Paranoid Android. He's always in a bad mood."

Corey nodded. "Yeah, except Marvin is funny. She's more like the captain of the Vogon Constructor Fleet, the one who writes all that terrible poetry and wants everyone to like it."

Rigel laughed. "You're right, she is. That's one of the best—"

She cut herself off. She looked around the table.

Three expectant faces looked back.

"*You* gave me that book. Corey, it was you!" The lightbulb finally switched on. "It was *all* of you!"

Sylvie nodded, and Sam laughed. Corey grinned and said, "Finally."

"But we didn't even know each other then."

Sylvie said, "It was kind of a group project. We thought you were an interesting p-p-person. And I could tell they were

233

getting you down. You can deal with Hayden and those people if you have a few friends. If you don't, it's hard."

Rigel wasn't surprised Sylvie had worked this out. In their group, Sam fed them, Corey stood up for them, and Sylvie watched. She noticed stuff.

Sylvie went on, "So we decided it was time for action."

"An act of rebellion against Hayden's senseless persecution," Corey said.

"A random act of kindness and senseless b-b-b-beauty." Sylvie wrinkled her nose. "That's what my mom calls it. Oh, it sounds corny, but you know what I mean."

"It wasn't corny. It was great."

"And we gave you *Hitchhiker's Guide* because it's Corey's favorite book and he made us all read it, so we figured it might save you time later." Sam took the last cream puff.

Rigel held up a finger. "Okay, something's been bugging me. Why did you leave it on Mrs. Green's chair, instead of my desk?"

Sam said, "Because then everyone would see her give it to you."

Sylvie beamed. "We knew that would make Hayden crazy."

"And it worked! She was obviously enraged!" Corey beamed too.

Rigel laughed. "You know, Blueberry liked that present too. It tried to drag away that ribbon first thing—" Blueberry, trying to be sneaky, dragging its shiny prize away . . . That memory was always going to make her happy.

She never would have known Blueberry if she hadn't come here.

Sylvie, Sam, or Corey either.

Rigel looked around the table. "Are we playing dominoes or what?"

Chapter 21

A few days later, Rigel had an email from Kimora. Not the usual complaints about being bored, or gossip from school, but something different.

Jeez, did I get in trouble, Kimora wrote.

Mom was ignoring me, so I knew she was mad about something I did. Then last night Paulette and your dad came over and Bear wanted to know everything I said to you last time we talked. I guess you didn't know about Prudhoe or Paulette or any of that! Mom said I've got the world's biggest mouth and I should be setting a better example for all the younger kids. She said it was Bear's business to tell you. But then I said maybe it was better for you to know and finally even Mom had to admit that was probably true. I still feel bad about it, though.

Bear says you're really mad at him. You know no matter what Bear does he's still your dad, right? I'd do anything to have my dad back again.

Rigel sat trying to write Kimora back. She either needed to write a long email or a short one, and she was struggling to get it right when someone behind her said, "Rigel."

It was Mrs. Green.

Rigel jumped. Then she fumbled to minimize her email screen before Mrs. Green could look over her shoulder and start critiquing sentences.

Mrs. Green had a way of making Rigel feel guilty even when she wasn't doing anything wrong.

"Sorry to startle you, but I have a favor to ask. Julie Han is sick, and she needs some books and her school assignments. Her mom called the office and asked if someone could drop them off at her house after school."

"Apartment," Rigel heard herself say.

"Excuse me?"

"They live in an apartment."

Mrs. Green sneezed into her elbow and took a Kleenex from her sweater pocket. Maybe she had caught Julie's cold herself. "Apartment, then. The point is, can you do it? Aren't you and Julie friends?"

What was Rigel supposed to say?

That they weren't?

She's not my friend, Rigel imagined saying. It was true. But it sounded so mean. Like something Hayden would say.

Besides, the Hans' store was barely out of her way home. She didn't even need to talk to Julie. She could just leave the bag for her.

So Rigel nodded. "I can't get into Julie's locker, though."

"They'll have the combination in the office. I'll get everything together for you. Just come by my room after school."

As Mrs. Green walked away, the bell rang. Rigel had to quit on her email to Kimora and get to class.

 ̶H̶H̶T̶

The big windows at Baldwin Stationery were so fogged up Rigel couldn't see inside. Moisture was condensing and rolling down the windows. The door jingled as she came in, and Mrs. Han got up from her stool behind the counter.

"Rigel! Long time! You kids stay so busy, don't you?"

"I've got Julie's books," Rigel said, lifting the bulging shopping bag for Mrs. Han to see.

"That's good! Go on up and say hi." Mrs. Han pointed toward the door at the back of the store.

"Maybe I could just—"

The phone rang and Mrs. Han picked it up. "Baldwin

Stationery. Yes . . . Yes, we have scented markers . . . A pack of thirty-six? Let me check, okay?"

Rigel went back through the store, with its familiar comforting smell of paper and ink, through the door, and up the stairs.

She could just leave the bag outside the apartment door. Although that would seem weird. Like she was scared, or something. *Oh, quit being such a baby,* Rigel told herself. The worst thing Julie could do was be a doink. And she'd done that already.

Rigel knocked on the door.

It opened right away. Julie must have been in the living room. Her nose was red and she was in pajamas and a pair of moose slippers.

Rigel lifted the bag. Julie took it.

"Thanks." She stood aside, inviting Rigel in.

A whiff of soup came through the open door. The smell was delicious on this cool day.

Rigel went in, and Julie shut the door behind her.

"How are you feeling?" Rigel asked.

If nothing else, they could at least talk about Julie's cold.

"My nose looks terrible, but I'm feeling a lot better. My mom made me bean sprout soup. It cures everything."

Loud music came from Danny's room. A hoarse voice screamed something out, and powerful chords thudded through the apartment.

"Danny's gotten into heavy metal. Every afternoon it's

like this now," Julie said. "You want some soup? It's spicy. Mom puts in tons of red pepper."

Rigel nodded and sat down at the table. Julie served up a bowl of soup and some rice from the rice cooker on the counter. A drawer rattled open and Julie pulled out a deep spoon and a pair of chopsticks. She put it all down in front of Rigel, and then got another helping for herself.

For a while they ate in silence. The food was delicious. Rigel's eyes and nose started streaming from the pepper, but she kept on eating anyway.

Julie slurped up a bean sprout. "How's Blueberry doing?"

Rigel choked on her soup and coughed before answering. It seemed like everyone at Fields Middle knew about Rigel Harman and her crow, but not many people knew that the crow had a name. "How did you know its name is Blueberry?"

"Sylvie told me. Hey, why do you call Blueberry 'it'—not 'he' or 'she'? That seems so weird."

"Because I can't tell what sex Blueberry is. It isn't easy to tell, unless you're watching courtship behavior, and that only happens in the spring. It's not even easy to tell one crow from another." Rigel tapped her nose. "I'm lucky Blueberry has that splotch."

"It just seems like you'd pick 'he' or 'she.'"

"Not if your mom was a biologist you wouldn't." Rigel thought of Lila's fussiness about the difference between "rabbit" and "hare."

"Maybe not."

The heavy metal stopped. Different music came on.

"Now he's playing this old band called Iron Butterfly." Julie shook her head. "My uncle Sung-min got Danny into it and now it's 'In-A-Gadda-Da-Vida' every single day. Anyway, how *is* Blueberry doing? You didn't tell me."

"It hates being in a cage. My mom says it bites the rehab guy, Kevin, whenever it gets the chance. But that's good, really. It means Blueberry's still wild. It's healing up really well."

"Your mom says? What do you mean? Don't you go see it?"

"Against the rules," Rigel said. Julie's eyes went wide. "I know."

"Can they *do* that to you? That blows!"

Julie's sympathy made Rigel feel better. Not many people understood what it was like not seeing Blueberry anymore and only hearing about how the bird was doing from Lila.

Rigel ate the last spoonful of her rice and looked again around the familiar room. There was a big black bag dumped behind the door. "What's that?"

"It's my fencing bag."

"How's fencing going? It sounded like a blast."

"It's even more fun than I thought it would be," Julie said.

Rigel looked again at the bag. "It sounded cool. I wanted to try it too, but—" She fell into an embarrassing silence. They both knew why Rigel hadn't done fencing.

Julie recovered her nerve first. "We've got a few more practices this year. I could ask Mr. Brodeur if you could come and watch. Maybe try out a few moves. I bet he'd say yes. He's already talking about how to grow the club."

Rigel considered this. What else did she have to do after school, now that Blueberry was gone? Besides, she had missed Julie. She had missed her directness and her funny, sharp comments about things.

"He wants us to give a demonstration during assembly." Julie jumped out of her chair and sank into a fencer's stance.

Rigel got up and did her best to stand the same way.

"Bend your knees, bend your knees . . . Feet into an L shape, farther apart . . . That's not bad."

Danny came in. "Are you kids having fun playing in here?" He tucked his hair behind his ears, opened the cupboard, and took out a soup bowl. "It's a little crowded for fencing, don't you think?"

Julie jabbed her imaginary épée at Danny's butt.

"I don't know what you're doing, but cut it out," Danny said, ladling soup into his bowl. That only made them laugh harder.

HHT

February in Connecticut was full of wet snow that fell and melted, fell again and then melted again.

Rigel unlocked the side door, her mind full of numbers. Not countdown numbers. She was thinking of Nature Club dues.

It was no wonder her friends had wanted her to attend the Nature Club organizational meeting. Before she even knew what was going on, she had been elected what Mr. Hernandez called "interim treasurer." (Tracee Waterston had moved to South Carolina and couldn't do it anymore.)

Now Rigel was figuring out how much activity money they would have for spring activities once snacks were deducted from the club budget. The answer was not much. Maybe they should do bake sales. Sam would be good at that.

She stepped inside their house, shook clumps of snow off her jacket over the mat, and took the jacket into the downstairs bathroom to hang over the sink and dry. Willow's and Izzy's coats were already there.

So Willow was home again, instead of being at Christian's.

That was happening more and more often lately.

Something thumped upstairs.

And now that Rigel was paying attention, there was another noise, a sort of whining roar. She went upstairs. The roar was coming from the hall bathroom. It sounded like a hair dryer. Was Izzy playing around in there?

Rigel knocked on the bathroom door. "Hello?"

The roar cut off. "*What?*" Willow said.

Had Willow washed her hair in the middle of the day? "Are you okay?" Rigel called.

"Oh, come in if you want," Willow said. "Everyone else is in here."

Inside the bathroom, Willow sat on the edge of the tub,

Judit stood by the sink blow-drying Willow's hair, and Izzy was squashed in between the window and the toilet, looking excited.

Willow's hair had a new streak of bubble-gum pink that started at one shoulder and spilled all the way down to her waist.

"Willow *striped* her hair," Izzy whispered.

"We could do you next," Judit offered. She had pink streaks in her hair that matched Willow's.

"Jay! We are *not* dying any middle school hair," Willow said. "And you can forget about it too," she said to Izzy.

"What will Christian think of it?" Rigel asked.

Willow and Judit looked at each other.

"Who cares what that muggle thinks?" Judit gathered up the trash from the sink—a box of hair dye, crumpled latex gloves, a ball of aluminum foil, and a mess of paper towels. "Could you give me a hand?" she asked Izzy, nodding at the plastic bowl streaked with hot-pink dye.

The two of them headed downstairs, Izzy chattering about the colors she would put in her own hair as soon as she could.

Willow peered in the mirror. She seemed surprised herself by the bright pink in her hair. "I can always cut it out if I decide I hate it. That's why we only did one streak."

"I like it," Rigel said. Not because she was sure she did, but because she guessed Willow needed cheering up.

"At least Christian will hate it," Willow said. "Oh, news flash. We broke up."

Should Rigel say she was sorry, even though she wasn't? "Are you okay?"

"I don't know." Willow grimaced. "At least now I can go to Art Club and have my own friends and dye my hair pink without getting his *permission* first." Willow turned back to the mirror, and this time swept her hair over her shoulder and twisted it so it looked like a braid. The pink streak ran through it like a ribbon. It was pretty that way. Then she frowned, leaned closer, and examined some flaw on her forehead.

Willow could go on for ages doing that kind of stuff, and she didn't appreciate an audience. So Rigel picked up her backpack and went to her room.

She unpacked her books and stacked up her homework from hardest to easiest. Then she went to the chest of drawers to change her shirt.

Willow's picture hung there. Rigel hadn't looked at it in a while.

She studied the scene in all its jewel-like details.

The little cloth Bear smiled out at her over his big yellow beard. She blocked him out with her thumb and stood back to look at the picture again.

But it wasn't right that way, not without Bear. She let her hand fall back to her side.

She wondered whether anyone even got out to their cabin anymore. Probably animals had gotten in by now and rummaged through everything and crapped on the floor the way they did. She could hardly stand to think of their cabin abandoned, even though there were lots of abandoned cabins in Alaska. Just a few miles upstream from their place there was an old tar-paper shack that Rigel, Willow, and Izzy used as a sort of fort. Someone had lived there once, but not even Bear remembered who, or what had happened.

"You can take it down, you know," Willow said. She was leaning up against the doorway jamb, watching. "It won't hurt my feelings."

Rigel shook her head.

Willow came over and they looked at the picture together. "When we first came Outside, all I remembered about that cabin were the awful things. Like packing water, and never having any money, and Bear and Lila fighting. But there was good stuff there too."

"The salmon was a lot better, for one thing."

"It was! But, Rye, come on. Connecticut isn't so bad."

She admitted, "It's not so terrible."

"Don't worry. Your secret is safe with me."

"Yeah, right."

Willow laughed. "Come on. Let's go downstairs and make some hot Tang. I bet Judit's never had it."

Rigel hesitated. Hot Tang was a bush thing, what you drank in the winter when you didn't have fresh orange juice and didn't want a cold drink anyway. Hot Tang was important. What if Judit thought it was gross and made fun of it?

"Judit might not like it," she said.

"Just because she doesn't like it doesn't mean that we can't like it," Willow said. "Why are you smiling like that?"

"Just because," Rigel said, and then gave Willow a hug. She caught Willow by surprise, with her arms down, but once her arms were free, she gave Rigel a hug in return.

The real Willow was back. Hopefully she'd stay awhile.

Chapter 22

Rigel and her sisters were eating dinner with Grandma when they heard the side door open and shut.

They heard the clatter of Lila putting down all the buckets and mops. Then a crackling sound that was Lila taking her wet raincoat off. It had been raining all day.

March in Connecticut could mean either rain or snow, according to Grandma. Lately it had been rain.

Grandma was starting seedlings on the dining room table, the winter quilts had been swapped out for thinner ones, and Lila was threatening them all with spring-cleaning.

Lila came back to the kitchen, picked up her plate, and went to the stove. She smelled like bleach.

"Sorry I'm late, but I have some good news. They're

calling me in for a second interview at that lab over in New Haven."

Lila had been job hunting for so long, Rigel sometimes forgot her mom was still looking.

"I have a good feeling about this one. They like the off-the-grid experience, instead of acting like it's something I should explain away. And, Rye Bear, I heard from Kevin Brecker. Guess what? He's releasing Blueberry next week."

"That's great!" Grandma said.

Blueberry was well enough to be released. The crow wasn't going to spend the rest of its life in a cage, the way Rigel sometimes felt like she was doing, even now.

It would be a better life for Blueberry.

Rigel was going to be glad for the crow even if it killed her.

Lila took a small spoonful of peas. They weren't her favorite vegetable. She always said she had eaten too many canned peas in Alaska.

"He's doing the release next Monday. You and I are going to have to be up even earlier than usual that day, Rigel."

Rigel forked in some meatloaf and started chewing before she realized what her mom had just said. She said through the mouthful, "He'sgoingtoletusbethere?"

"Rigel! That's gross!" Izzy shouted.

"That depends. I told Kevin we would follow every one of his rules, and he's got a list about half a mile long. No calling to Blueberry, no sneaking treats, no asking him to pose for pictures. Kevin hates that as much as you do. We sit nice and quiet and watch. Can you do that?"

Rigel nodded.

Willow said, "I've seen videos of crow releases. Some people make a big deal out of it. They let tons of people watch, and they film the whole thing, and everyone claps when the bird flies off—"

"That's not the way Kevin does it, and this is his show."

"I want to go too," Izzy protested.

"Okay, Iz, that's fine. I'll wake you at five thirty. That's when Rigel and I are getting up."

"Never mind," Izzy mumbled. She hated getting up early in the morning. She was a Connecticut kid now.

卌

When Rigel got up on Monday, she could smell eggs and bacon from downstairs. Her breakfast was ready on the table and Lila was drinking coffee. They drove toward Naugatuck in the dark. It was too early for chatting.

Kevin lived in a small farmhouse with a barn and a row of tumbledown greenhouses behind it. He came out to greet them with a mug of tea in one hand and slippers on his feet.

"See those oaks over there, next to the barn? Go stand there, and keep quiet." He looked Rigel over. Something about the way he examined her, looking for anything and everything wrong, reminded her of Mrs. Green. "And zip up your jacket. That shirt is too bright. The crow will see it from a mile away."

Rigel zipped up her jacket and she and Lila went to stand under the trees, dodging crumbling pats of cow manure.

Kevin came out from the greenhouse carrying a cardboard box taped shut. SALERNO IMPORTERS. It was Sam's box, from all that time ago.

He crouched down in front of it. He was using a jackknife or something similar to cut the tape. Then he opened the flaps and stood back.

A crow bulleted out of the box to the top of a tree snag.

"Blueberry," Rigel muttered.

"Hush," Lila whispered.

Blueberry looked strong and glossy. It perched with confidence, up high, where it should be. It settled its wings and cocked its head, looking around. It flew farther away from Kevin and landed in another tree. *Caw-caw!*

Some crows called back from nearby. Blueberry raised its head, listening, and returned the greeting.

Rigel put her hands over her mouth the way Izzy did when she needed to stay quiet.

Blueberry flicked its tail, shifted its weight from foot to foot, and flew up higher, out onto the tip of a leafing branch. The sun was behind the crow now and Rigel could barely see it.

Then Blueberry flew back to the snag.

The crow turned its head, looking in their direction.

It flew closer. This time it landed on a fence not far from the barn.

"What's it doing?" Lila whispered.

Blueberry turned its head. It was looking at Rigel. This time she was sure of it.

Kr-rrr, Blueberry rattled.

"Rigel," Lila said warningly, but Rigel's knees were bending without her wanting them to. She knelt down in the muddy spring grass and Blueberry landed in front of her.

"Blueberry."

It wasn't exactly like their old days together. Blueberry stayed farther back than it once would have done and didn't take its gaze off her. Rigel knew to move slowly. She reached out cautiously and scratched the crow's head.

Kr-rrr. Mmmm.

"You're looking nice and strong. I guess Kevin took good care of you, huh?"

Blueberry grabbed her finger in its bill, then gave her a hard nip on the hand.

"Ow! I know you're mad, but it wasn't my fault." Rigel blinked back tears of pain. "It wasn't my idea. They just took you away. No one asked me what I thought about it."

Blueberry stretched its wings and flapped before settling back down to relaxed alertness. It spared a look toward the trees and shifted from foot to foot. Rigel recognized the uncertain look of a traveler at an airport—someone who didn't want to leave a friend, but knew there was a plane to catch.

She sat back on her heels and put her hands on her knees so Blueberry could see where they were.

"I guess you need to get going, huh?"

Mmmmm, Blueberry murmured.

"You're going to be fine, you know that? You do know that already. Show-off."

But Blueberry still didn't fly. It shifted restlessly.

Rigel held out her finger once more and the crow grabbed it in its bill. It held on a long moment before letting go.

Then Blueberry spread its wings and sprang into the air.

This time the crow flew fast and far, up over the field and into the trees on the other side. It landed on a telephone pole, cawed briefly, got another answer, and flew away over the woods.

Blueberry was gone.

||||

"That went well," Lila said.

"Uh-huh."

They were back in the car, driving east toward home. Rigel stared out at the highway shoulder, littered with trash, everything from fast-food bags to collapsed cardboard boxes and shreds of tire.

Lila went on. "Blueberry looked good and strong. Didn't you think?"

Rigel nodded.

"Did you hear all those crows calling it? I bet that bird's going to do just fine."

"Uh-huh."

The car tires hummed over the asphalt.

Blueberry might be meeting its new crow family right now. Rigel hoped the other crows were being nice, not pecking and bullying like corvids sometimes did. She hoped Blueberry could hold its own.

Lila sighed. "The sun is right in my eyes." She flipped down her visor and turned on the radio.

"I miss Blueberry," Rigel said.

"It seems like Blueberry missed you too." It was unlike Lila to say something like that. She didn't approve of people talking about animals as if they had human emotions. "Anthropomorphism," she called it.

"You think so?"

"It certainly remembered you. It trusted you. If Kevin ever tried to scratch Blueberry on its head, he'd get a good bite for the trouble." She chuckled and then turned serious. "I know it wasn't easy for you, Rigel, that Blueberry went away, and I'm proud of the way you handled it. Actually, I'm proud of how you've handled this whole year."

Really? Lila thought that?

"I knew it would be hard on you, leaving our place. You loved it there so much."

Rigel looked past the grimy highway at the fields and scattered houses on both sides. Plenty of open spaces and trees, the occasional garbage can . . . Her mom was right. This was a good place for a crow.

"Hey, Lila. Do you think I'll ever go back to Alaska?"

"You will, someday, if you want it badly enough. I'm sure of that." Lila reached over and tugged one of Rigel's braids. "Until then, you'll just have to keep the Alaska alive inside yourself."

Chapter 23

A beautiful spring day in May meant that there were a lot of people at the scenic overlook. Most of them were sneezing because the ground was covered with golden-brown lumps of tree pollen.

The ravens didn't care who was watching them. Maybe they liked the audience, knowing they were safe from anything other than hawks and eagles. They were up to all kinds of wild flying out there.

Lila watched them with a grin. She was in a good mood. She liked her new job at the lab and lately she was saying that things had "settled down" at home.

Willow sat on a big rock, sketching.

Rigel walked to the edge of the overlook and shielded her eyes. "Drop me a pack."

It was what Wilfred had always said when he saw ravens playing in midair.

Lila gave a low chuckle. "Do you think those ravens are Athabascan, Rigel?"

"Lila, look!" Rigel yelled.

The biggest raven did a half roll, like it was dumping a heavy knapsack off its back.

Lila blinked. "I take it back. Maybe they are Athabascan after all."

"Sophie must have talked to them," Willow suggested. "She called them up on the raven telephone and said, 'I need you to help someone for me.' "

That was Sophie, all right. She was always trying to help out someone who needed it.

"Anyway, it's Rigel's birthday, so of course she's getting a pack." Willow slapped her sketchbook shut and shoved it under her arm.

"The ravens probably know it." Lila nodded. "And speaking of birthdays, we need to get home and finish getting ready for the party."

Rigel took one last look at the ravens before following Lila and Willow down the well-worn path, slippery with spring mud.

HHT

There were so many people in the house for dinner that they ate in the dining room instead of the kitchen. Corey, Sam, Sylvie, and Julie all came.

Lila made rabbit casserole.

Rigel had warned her friends ahead of time, in case some of them didn't like rabbit, but they all at least tried some. (Although Sylvie didn't eat more than a few bites.)

"Happy birthday to you, happy birthday to you—"

Lila brought the carrot cake to the table, its twelve candles already burning.

"—happy birthday, dear Riiiiiigel, happy birthday to you!"

Rigel blew out the candles with one long, steady breath.

"Rigel, tell us what you wished for!"

"She can't *do* that. Then it won't come true."

This was the best moment of Rigel's birthday every year, the moment when the singing of "Happy Birthday" was finally over and she could start eating cake.

She sat down and picked up her fork, and then Lila reached under the table and whisked out a box. "Surprise!"

A little greasy box, postmarked Fort McPhee, Alaska. Bear's return address was written in a woman's handwriting.

Rigel could smell what was inside. They usually opened presents after eating cake, but this one time she couldn't wait. She grabbed her table knife and, before Grandma could mention respect for the good silver, slit open the top of the box. She lifted out the thick plastic bag, heavy with dark orange sticks.

"What *is* that?" Julie asked, staring.

"Salmon strips!" Izzy shouted.

"It's salmon jerky," Lila explained.

"It must be an Alaska thing," Corey said, sniffing.

The salmon's rich smell filled the dining room and made Rigel's mouth water. "Let's all have a piece. We can share it."

"Wow," Willow said. "Rigel really does love us, Izzy. She's sharing her salmon strips."

The jerky was good, although of course it had been made from last summer's salmon run and that meant it was a little dried out, less fresh than Rigel preferred. She wondered who had made it. Paulette? A friend of Paulette? Maybe it was Sophie who had cut this fish and seasoned it and hung it up on a rack to dry. It was still Rigel's favorite food, whoever had made it. That was another thing that was not going to change. It was going to be one of those pieces of Alaska that she would carry inside herself, always.

"Salmon jerky and birthday cake." Sam half closed his eyes while he chewed. "This is working for me."

꜀꜀꜀꜀꜀꜀

That night Rigel had trouble sleeping. She was excited and tired at the same time, and something else she couldn't name.

She lay awake, staring up at the ceiling.

Finally, she crept down to the kitchen, where the black-cat clock said 1:00. Rigel had a drink of water at the sink, looking out at the night sky. At least it wasn't orange tonight.

It wasn't the right time of year to see Orion, but she could see stars overhead.

Rigel felt like she was waiting for something, and after a while she knew what it was.

She dialed Bear's number. She remembered it. Rigel had trouble remembering how to spell "tomorrow," but a nine-digit number stuck in her head like a burr.

The phone rang and this time Bear answered.

"Hi, Dad," Rigel said.

Why had she called him "Dad"? She never called him that.

"Rigel?" Bear said. "Well—how's the birthday girl?"

So this is how he was going to play it. Like that last conversation of theirs had never happened.

"I just wanted to say thanks for the jerky."

"No problem. Paulette got all that together for me."

The name "Paulette" punched into her ear like a hammered-down nail, but, after all, it was the truth. And Bear went right on talking anyway.

"You're getting all grown-up now—twelve years old!"

"I guess."

What did Bear expect? For her to get younger, or stay eleven forever?

"Your mom said you were having a party, and your friends were all going to come . . ." His voice trailed off.

Rigel didn't know what to say. Oh, she could tell him about the party, about Grandma's spring gardening, even about how things were going at school, but why? What was the point?

Bear said, his voice quieter than usual, "Look, kid. I know I let you down."

Rigel was pretty sure she heard him swallow.

"I made some promises I shouldn't have. I wanted to believe it so much myself, I guess. And then, when things started up with Paulette, I just didn't know what to say."

"Okay," Rigel said. She understood that. The not knowing what to say.

"It would have been better to say something . . ." Bear began, and then stopped. She waited for him to go on from there, but he didn't. This was what she was going to get. Still, it was more than she'd expected. It was kind of an apology. And it was a whole lot better than Bear just pretending he hadn't done anything wrong and didn't know what she was mad about. That used to happen a lot with Lila.

"I'm going to join the Fencing Club next year at school," Rigel heard herself say.

"Fencing?" Bear sounded surprised. Also relieved. "You mean, like in pirate movies? Well, cool."

"And I'm in the Nature Club now. Me and my friends."

"That doesn't surprise me so much," Bear said.

And then they did talk for a while about stuff like Grandma's daffodils, and Rigel's birthday, and the ravens at the overlook. Also about Paulette, and the spring hunting, and how Bear was trying to get a custodian job at the village school.

"I ought to get going, kiddo," her father said.

"Bear? Maybe you could start calling us once in a while? Willow and Izzy would like that too."

She could tell by her father's silence that she had pushed it. But if you couldn't do that on your birthday, when could you?

"I'll take it under advisement," he said at last. "Now, get your behind off to bed. I'm still your father, you know."

"I love you, Bear."

"I love you too." He added quickly, "I'll try to start calling on Sundays," before hanging up.

They still had a lot to catch up on, but at least they had made a start.

Rigel cut herself a big piece of birthday cake and carried it into the dining room. Munching, she looked out the windows at their empty street. Then she opened the side door with her free hand and took her cake out onto the stoop.

Outside it was cool and damp. She went over and inspected the young plants in the garden and then walked to the curb and looked up and down their street just for the pleasure of seeing it quiet and dark.

Of course, it wasn't *really* quiet and dark. She heard a car zoom by a few blocks away. Down the block, someone's furnace came on with a click and a hum. Dr. Morgan always had his porch light on, day and night. And that wasn't even counting all their streetlights.

Still, it wasn't bad.

A square of yellow appeared beside her on the grass.

She turned back and glanced up at the windows of Grandma's house.

Lila's light was on, and she stood at the window in her pajamas. She lifted one hand.

Rigel waved back. She held up the chunk of birthday cake and took a huge bite.

She could see Lila laugh.

Then Lila waved once more and disappeared from the window. Her light went out.

Rigel crammed the rest of the cake into her mouth and licked the frosting off her hand. She was going to have to brush her teeth again, but it had been totally worth it.

She took one more look around and then climbed their stoop. She wiped her bare feet on the mat and went back inside, where everyone else was in bed. She remembered to lock the door.

She went slowly and quietly up the stairs.

She wasn't in a hurry. She had time to sleep in.

Rigel had all the time she needed now.

Acknowledgments

This book would not be what it is without the advice and edits of Nova Ren Suma, Carrie Jones, and Bethany Hegedus. Bethany in particular read draft after draft without ever losing her patience or enthusiasm. I owe her a great deal. Other thoughtful readers include Margaret Meacham and Francisco Stork. Without all that help, this book may never have found its way to Rachel Orr, dedicated agent, steely-eyed editor, and hilarious companion, and to editor extraordinaire Erica Finkel at Abrams. Rob Sternitzky did a fantastic job copyediting this manuscript, and Maeve Norton's book cover was everything I dreamed of, only better. Many thanks to you all.

Bird-loving friends Evan Cutler, Renee Moffett Thompson, and Renee's husband, the late Steve Thompson, pointed me to good corvid resources, brainstormed possible outcomes, and patiently answered many, many (so very many!) nitpicky questions. Lauren Adams at the Vermont Institute of Natural Science shared her expertise on bird rehabilitation. Once again, thank you. The generous ladies of FTFriends answered question after question about everything from KenKen puzzles to current slang, lockers to lunchrooms. XOXOXO

The helpful folks at SCBWI Alaska hooked me up with Tricia Brown, long-time Alaska resident and writer, who gave the book an Alaska read and saved me from some howlers. Thanks, Tricia. Angela Gonzalez, creator and author of the *Athabascan Woman Blog*, also gave the book a thorough read and spared me a lot of embarrassment. *Enna baasee'*, Angela.

Old friends Trudy Lewis and John Picard were honest, supportive, and kind. You are both rare people, and anyone who has you for a friend is lucky. Other friends whose encouragement extended beyond the call of duty include Susan Cohen, Peggy Duggan, and Jennifer Richmond. Friends Jill Kimball and Tom Wittmann helped me out often in the most practical way possible—by babysitting.

My husband, Bill Moran, gave support in ways large and small, acting as cheerleader and counselor with just the occasional necessary smidgen of drill sergeant. He sets his own good example of hard work, dedication, and humor. My son, Nick, inspires me every day to do my best, the same way he does. I love you both.

My father, Al Carr, was stationed on Kodiak Island during the Korean War and his descriptions, stories, and photos started me dreaming about Alaska at an early age. John McPhee's book *Coming into the Country* cemented that interest into a committed fascination, so I named a Koyukon Indian village for him. Fort McPhee is a fictional place, along with Baldwin, Connecticut. The made-up Lee Price Chappell Wilderness is named for three of my writing teachers, Reynolds Price, Fred Chappell, and Lee Zacharias. While we're at it, you will not find the Birch Grove overlook on any map, although it's true that ravens have returned to the state of Connecticut. Long may they remain.

I wrote this book. That means I am the one responsible for any errors or mistakes concerning corvids, wildlife rehabilitation, Athabascan Indian languages and cultures, and Alaska's complicated geography, culture, history, and culinary heritage, including hot Tang recipes. And the same goes for Connecticut.

About the Author

Cathy Carr grew up in Wisconsin, where a steady supply of her dad's stories about his Alaskan adventures sparked her interest in the forty-ninth state. A former copyeditor, library clerk, and technical writer, she now lives in New Jersey with her family and writes fiction. In her spare time, she quilts, cooks, reads, and hikes—among other things. *365 Days to Alaska* is her first novel.